Cowboy at Heart

SHIPMENT ONE

Tex Times Ten by Tina Leonard
Runaway Cowboy by Judy Christenberry
Crazy for Lovin' You by Teresa Southwick
The Rancher Next Door by Cathy Gillen Thacker
Intimate Secrets by B.J. Daniels
Operation: Texas by Roxanne Rustand

SHIPMENT TWO

Navarro or Not by Tina Leonard
Trust a Cowboy by Judy Christenberry
Taming a Dark Horse by Stella Bagwell
The Rancher's Family Thanksgiving by Cathy Gillen Thacker
The Valentine Two-Step by RaeAnne Thayne
The Cowboy and the Bride by Marin Thomas

SHIPMENT THREE

Catching Calhoun by Tina Leonard
The Christmas Cowboy by Judy Christenberry
The Come-Back Cowboy by Jodi O'Donnell
The Rancher's Christmas Baby by Cathy Gillen Thacker
Baby Love by Victoria Pade
The Best Catch in Texas by Stella Bagwell
This Kiss by Teresa Southwick

SHIPMENT FOUR

Archer's Angels by Tina Leonard
More to Texas than Cowboys by Roz Denny Fox
The Rancher's Promise by Jodi O'Donnell
The Gentleman Rancher by Cathy Gillen Thacker
Cowboy's Baby by Victoria Pade
Having the Cowboy's Baby by Stella Bagwell

SHIPMENT FIVE

Belonging to Bandera by Tina Leonard
Court Me, Cowboy by Barbara White Daille
His Best Friend's Bride by Jodi O'Donnell
The Cowboy's Return by Linda Warren
Baby Be Mine by Victoria Pade
The Cattle Baron by Margaret Way

SHIPMENT SIX

Crockett's Seduction by Tina Leonard
Coming Home to the Cattleman by Judy Christenberry
Almost Perfect by Judy Duarte
Cowboy Dad by Cathy McDavid
Real Cowboys by Roz Denny Fox
The Rancher Wore Suits by Rita Herron
Falling for the Texas Tycoon by Karen Rose Smith

SHIPMENT SEVEN

Last's Temptation by Tina Leonard
Daddy by Choice by Marin Thomas
The Cowboy, the Baby and the Bride-to-Be by Cara Colter
Luke's Proposal by Lois Faye Dyer
The Truth About Cowboys by Margot Early
The Other Side of Paradise by Laurie Paige

SHIPMENT EIGHT

Mason's Marriage by Tina Leonard
Bride at Briar's Ridge by Margaret Way
Texas Bluff by Linda Warren
Cupid and the Cowboy by Carol Finch
The Horseman's Son by Delores Fossen
Cattleman's Bride-to-Be by Lois Faye Dyer

The rugged, masculine and independent men
of America's West know the value of hard work,
honor and family. They may be ranchers, tycoons
or the guy next door, but they're all cowboys at heart.
Don't miss any of the books in this collection!

Cowboy
at
Heart

NAVARRO OR NOT

TINA LEONARD

USA TODAY Bestselling Author

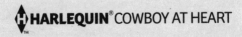

HARLEQUIN® COWBOY AT HEART

Recycling programs
for this product may
not exist in your area.

ISBN-13: 978-0-373-82608-7

NAVARRO OR NOT

Copyright © 2004 by Tina Leonard

Printed in U.S.A.

TINA LEONARD

is a *USA TODAY* bestselling author of more than forty projects, including a popular thirteen-book miniseries for Harlequin American Romance. Her books have made the Waldenbooks, Ingram and Nielsen BookScan bestseller lists. Tina feels she has been blessed with a fertile imagination and quick typing skills, excellent editors and a family who loves her career. Born on a military base, she lived in many states before eventually marrying the boy who did her crayon printing for her in the first grade. Tina believes happy endings are a wonderful part of a good life. You can visit her at www.tinaleonard.com.

To Lisa and Dean, always. I love you.
To my gal pals, whose friendship means so much to me:
Cryna Palmiere, Riza Majerreis, Donna Opalenik,
Jerry Shriver, Latesha Ballard, Amina Rusk,
Nicki Flockton, Jennifer, Sally Grabham
and KraziKim55!
And to my editors, who are excellent.
Many thanks to Paula Eykelhof and Stacy Boyd,
who have great patience and
who keep me doing what I love best.

Chapter One

Actions speak louder than words. So think your actions over many times.
—Maverick Jefferson when his boys got caught stealing Shoeshine Johnson's bus for a road trip because it was the only vehicle all twelve of them could fit into at once.

"What has to be done," Navarro Jefferson told his twin, Crockett, as they sat in his truck, "is that one of us should go live in Lonely Hearts Station. As a sort-of mole. To keep an eye on Last's pregnancy matter before it gets further out of hand."

Recently, Last, the youngest Jefferson brother and the family philosophe, had managed to get himself into trouble with a gal of questionable reputation from the wrong side of the beautician tracks.

Ever since their elder brother Frisco Joe had courted and married a stylist from the Lonely Hearts Salon—and put the Jefferson brothers in the middle of a duel between the Lonely Hearts beauties and their salon rivals, the Never Lonely Cut-n-Gurls—life had not been going well for any of the boys from Union Junction.

Not for Last, nor for the rest of his brothers.

Navarro had sort of expected more trouble, but lacking condom sense was not supposed to be in the cards.

"How would we do that?" Crockett asked. "I think the Never Lonely Cut-n-Gurls would know we were watching their every move."

"The only one we need to watch is Valentine," Navarro told his twin. "You and I could swap out, take turns, and they'd never know the difference. Tag-team girl-watching."

Crockett blinked. "Why do I find that appealing in a warped kind of way?" He considered the notion, peering out the truck window toward the Never Lonely Cut-n-Gurls salon. "Or possibly, I find it depressing. It's been a long time since I've had a woman."

"Whoa," Navarro said. "Too much info."

"Last says he doesn't remember anything about that night except that he was drinking some exceptional firewater."

"Man, I remember every good night I've had with a lady," Navarro bragged. "Even in my dreams."

"More there than not."

Navarro pulled his hat low over his eyes without comment.

"So how do we invade the landscape without raising suspicions? We need to get on the inside of that salon," Crockett said.

"Yeah. But bed maneuvers are out. I think there's enough trouble in the family tree when it comes to the ladies."

"Mmm." Crockett studied the goings-on of an attractive band of giggling Never Lonely girls as they left the salon. They were all dressed provocatively, which he appreciated. He wouldn't date any of the girls—not his type—but he certainly appreciated the goodness they were lending to the view. "You could dress in drag and become a hairdresser alongside them."

"I think not."

"You could become a client."

"I think they'd suspect my motives."
Everyone in town knew that the Jefferson
brothers were more likely to be seen at the
Lonely Hearts Salon across the street when
they needed a trim.

Crockett was silent for a moment. "You
could hit on Valentine."

"I'd rather gnaw off my leg. Anyway,
that would *totally* raise suspicions."

"Well, then you'd have to prove that your
intentions were honest, in order to get the
most info out of her. You'd have to get engaged."

Navarro laughed. "Right."

"*We* could get engaged. If we tag-team
spy, we might as well tag-team engage. No
one would notice that we were switching
out. And then we'd be on the *inside*."

"What a novel idea. Why don't we just
do something so stupid?"

"I'm serious." Crockett sat up straight.
"It's not very heroic, and it's deceitful, but
it would get us in a primo position to find
out the info we need to save our bro from
Valentine's catch-a-cowboy plot."

"We've done a lot worse, but I don't think Fannin would approve, even in the name of family. And when Mason comes home, he'd roast us for sure."

"I say it's easier to ask forgiveness than to get permission."

"I say…you've got a point." Navarro drummed the steering wheel. "How are we going to figure out which of those love-lies we want to sucker?"

"I don't know. How about the little plus-size gal over there with the pretty smile?"

"I think you may be looking at her chest when you talk 'plus size.' We could toss her between us like a doll. She's a little bitty thing—isn't she?—all curves and swerves."

"I like blondes," Crockett mused. "And she's not dressed fakey. She's kind of cute. Personality-wise, of course. Is there any chance we could reconsider sleeping with our girlfriend?"

"Absolutely not!" Navarro exclaimed.

"Rats. I do tend to fall easily to temptation. I really like a nice ripe bottom on a woman. She looks like she's all peach and no pit."

"She's definitely ripe. Hey, she's coming over! Turn your head and act like you're lost!"

"Hey, guys," the blonde said. "Lost?"

"Yes," Crockett said, because Navarro had pulled his hat over his face. "But we want to figure it out ourselves, if you know what I mean."

"Oh. You're adventurous types," she said.

"You could say that," Crockett agreed.

Nina Cakes smiled at the cowboy, realizing at once that here was the answer to her prayers.

"I need a man," she said.

"We've heard that before, sister," the cowboy told her. "And we're always ready to heed the call."

Nina took a step back from his leer. "Uh, cool your jets, cowboy. I said I need a man, not a mistake."

The man under the hat snickered. Nina went around to the driver's side to talk through the window. "Look, it's actually quite simple. I just need help lifting some boards up the stairs."

She frowned when he didn't answer.

"Navarro's resting. My brother tires out easily. By the way, I'm Crockett."

He stretched a hand across his brother for her to shake, which Nina did, reluctantly, trying to overlook the coughing fit that seemed to have possessed Hat Man. "He doesn't *look* like he's resting," she said. "Maybe when he gets up from his nap, I could offer him a job."

Crockett stretched his muscles for her. "'Course, I'm alive and kicking and ready to do your bidding. I can move a few pieces of wood—for free. I'd be *happy* to do it for such a pretty girl."

Nina tried not to roll her eyes. What a come-on! Did she look like the kind of girl who fell for an easy line? Librarians were far smarter than that, and she prided herself on being one of the most qualified, sharpest librarians in Dannon, Delaware.

Of course, today she was in a place called Lonely Hearts Station, Texas, with an heirloom bed her sister Valentine claimed had been broken accidentally. Nina pursed her lips and considered Crockett. He didn't exactly seem wholesome. What were the odds she could trust

him to help her without trying to paw her?
Far too sure of himself, he was quite different from the bookish, studious types who
came into her library: some students, some
older supporters of the library, an occa-
sional mom or dad—but nothing like this
man or his mysterious brother.

More wolf than sheep, for certain.

She'd bet these two were probably a
lot like the man who'd gotten her sister
into trouble. Valentine was in the family
way by a nefarious, no-good, irresponsible cowboy. If he was anything like these
men, no wonder Valentine had been lured
astray. Poor Valentine!

But first things first—the heirloom bed
was the matter at hand. Now that Nina had
come to Lonely Hearts Station to help her
sister, she needed a place to sleep. More
importantly, Nina would never be at ease
until the heirloom bed that had been in
their family for generations was repaired.

The bed was charmed. Nina stared at
the hat-covered face next to her, thinking
about the importance of the charm. What
would this man know about a woman's
secret desires? Every single member of

their female family had been conceived or born in that bed. The antique was simply magical in some way no one could really understand. Perhaps it was the delicate latticework headboard. Maybe the fine linens, which were more than a hundred years old, and the hand-crocheted lace edgings worked by Great-grandmother Eugenia from England.

Or the charm could simply rest in the bed's beauty and simple elegance. It invited a couple to share their dreams and joys while on its frame.

More than anything, Nina wanted that charm to work for her. One day, in the future. Certainly not in the way poor Valentine had chosen. Clearly the charm was still in serious good form because Valentine was due in about six months, give or take a week or two.

She sighed. "This is really important. I can't trust my bed to just anyone."

It seemed the cowboy under the hat got very still, his muscles bunching under his T-shirt. That man was no more resting than she was, Nina realized. He was awake and listening to every word she said.

The word "bed" really seemed to get his attention, she noticed.

Cowboys! Apparently they were only interested in boots, babes and beds.

Well, life just wasn't as carefree for her. "I'm going inside now," Nina said. "My room is upstairs. Number five. The wood for the slats is by the front door where the delivery company left it. I am in a desperate position, I will admit, so..." She looked at Crockett uncertainly. "Can you lift heavy things?"

"Of course," he said, sitting straight up. "Wood is my specialty. Lift, saw, nail, glue, hammer—"

"All right," Nina said. "Tell the woman at the desk that it's all right for you to go upstairs. Her name is Valentine."

"Valentine?" Crockett repeated, his tone surprised.

"I admit it's an unusual name, but then, one might say Crockett and Navarro are unusual, as well," Nina said. "My name is Nina Cakes. Nina is short for Eugenia. I'm named after my great-grandmother whose heirloom bed I am trying to repair. Valentine is my sister."

She noticed Navarro's posture became even more rigid. The stillest she'd ever seen in a human body. His fingers were clamped around the steering wheel bottom, just over his lap and right next to a large belt buckle. All cowboy. He smelled wonderful, she noticed on the sudden breeze that blew through the open windows of the truck. She stopped herself from giving an automatic "mmm" reaction and backed away. "Tell Valentine. I'll be upstairs," she said. "And please observe the house rules."

"Which would be?" Crockett called after her as she walked toward the salon.

"No talking to the women without an appointment," Nina said, and went inside, wondering what the man behind the hat had been hiding.

Elusive devil.

Poor Valentine. "You should have stayed up north," she told her sister grumpily as she walked past the reception area. "Clearly cowboys are just out for one thing."

"That's what we like about them," another hairstylist called. "Didn't you read the motto?"

Nina glanced at the glittery sign for the

hundredth time, high on the wall, with big letters. "'Save a horse, ride a cowboy,'" she muttered. "I can read, thanks."

She could also heed a warning.

"DUDE! THIS IS TOO EASY!" Crockett said, poking Navarro in the arm. "Drag those boards upstairs!"

"Slow down," Navarro said, the voice of caution. "We need to think this through."

"Think! Whatever happened to the man of action?"

Navarro pulled his hat off his face to look at his twin. "The man of action was the one not wearing a condom, drinking suspicious firewater and having a real good time. Which is why we're sitting here, instead of back in Union Junction at the ranch, where we belong. So, let's take a deep breath and consider the angles."

Crockett thumped his head back against the headrest. "Angle on."

"She scares me, for starters."

Crockett glanced over at him. "Scares you?"

"Yeah." Navarro shifted uncomfortably. "She's cute. She's got a sexy voice. It's kind of prim-and-proper don't-mess-with-me. I think my call of the wild found that to be an invitation."

Crockett laughed. "She had the hots for me, in case you didn't notice."

"I did not notice that." Navarro stared down the old road that was the center of Lonely Hearts Station. It separated one side of town from the other—and effectively separated the two battling beauty salons: Lonely Hearts Salon and the Never Lonely Cut-n-Gurls.

The Jefferson brothers owed a lot to Delilah, the owner of the Lonely Hearts Salon. She and her employees had chipped in to save Union Junction during the last big freeze. Delilah's sister, Marvella, was her arch nemesis, and was trying to put her out of business by selling, if rumor was to believed, something more than garden-variety mow-n-go haircuts at the Never Lonely Cut-n-Gurls salon. "Why did you tell her our real names?"

Crockett shrugged. "I didn't tell her our last names. Besides, she won't know who we are. You carry the boards up—"

"Why me?"

"Because you're the one sitting over there twitching for some action. You're the man with the call of the wild going on. Besides, you're more cautious than me. We both know I'd do something wrong."

"Impulsive."

"And rightfully so," Crockett said. "Come on, we haven't busted up a joint in months. We've had to mind our p's and q's with Mason taking off. Fannin running the joint. Mimi in the family way. The housekeeper taking over our house." Crockett blew out a breath. "Last going insane. I mean, I'm about tired of my p's and q's being so minded. I want our old life back. Before it got so reputation-conscious."

Navarro shook his head. "Valentine's sitting at the desk. She's going to recognize that we look an awful lot like the rest of the family."

Crockett shrugged. "Keep your hat low. Dump the lumber and go. But see if Valentine's really got a belly on her, or if that's just a bunch of bull to rope Last. I bet she's not even pregnant. And how do we know Last is the father? I mean, this *blows*." Crockett pulled his hat down over his face. "When this is all over, I'm going to go find Mason and tell him he's never gonna learn what happened to our father, and that he needs to deal with the fact that his true-love Mimi got married on him because he dragged his own dang boots, and that he needs to get his butt *home*."

"Good luck," Navarro said. "But first things first."

WHEN THE COWBOY WALKED into her room, Nina's blood started moving around in her body the way it never had before. A crazy tickle and then a full-blown rush filled her veins.

No, she told herself. Not this one. Completely inappropriate choice! *And there have been enough of those lately.* "Thanks for coming up," she said.

"There was no one at the desk," Navarro said. "I just made my way upstairs and—" His dark eyes swept her as she sat on the floor, a pencil and metal measuring tape in her hands. "What are you doing?"

"Measuring off," Nina said. "Highly advisable if I want to cut these slats properly."

He eyed the collapsed bed, which made

Nina's face blush a bit. Of course, it was hot in her room. A small fan blew nearby, but it was spring and Marvella hadn't turned the air-conditioning on yet because the nights were still cool. All the measuring and sawing was making her hot, Nina decided.

"Now that I've found your room, I'm going to go get the rest of the wood." Navarro backed away from her and Nina realized she probably looked sweaty and dirty.

"Thank you, Crockett."

He hesitated, then left. Nina took a deep breath, then jumped to her feet to cross to the mirror. Yes, sweaty and messy. "How did they make it in the good ol' days without air-conditioning? I'm going to fry my Delaware skin." Taking a damp rag, she swept it over her, then reached for some peach gloss to touch to her lips.

She was taking a few swipes at her hair in an effort to tame it when the cowboy strode in, carrying the lumber. Her gaze met his and she dropped the brush, embarrassed to be caught primping.

He grinned at her. "Nice."

That evil blooming of her skin she'd

felt moments before now blushed over her body in a heat wave no air conditioner would cool. She raised her chin. "You can set the wood down there."

His grin widened to wolfish. "You are a snappy little peach, I'll grant you that."

She couldn't take her eyes off him as he smoothly bent to rest the wood on the floor. His jeans fit so tightly, his butt looked so—

Glancing up, he caught her staring—and laughed.

"I've never seen a cowboy up this close," she said.

"Really? I've never seen a…what are you, anyway?"

"Librarian," Nina said, her chin rising, knowing already what he was going to say. "And I should warn you, I've heard every bad line about librarians you could possibly dream—"

"Now, I've heard that there are two kinds of librarians," the cowboy said, leaning up against the wall, his boots crossed, his arms tucked over his chest. His grin was too wide and too playful, and she longed to smack it off his face.

"Well, there is really only one kind of librarian," she said. "Serious."

"I heard there was also the skank variety."

She dropped the measuring tape she'd picked up. "'Skank variety'?"

"Yeah." He grinned. "She hovers in her book stacks, waiting for the right victim to come along so she can read him the Kama Sutra—well, 'read' would be the incorrect verb, I guess. And then—" he lowered his voice "—and then she seduces him in the basement, where he is never heard from again. Skank librarian." He shrugged. "That's where the haunted library story comes from. Haunted, you see, because it was the librarian who, like a black widow spider, kills her lover after they—"

"That is ridiculous! And so…chauvinistic!"

He laughed. "Bet you thought I was gonna repeat the stereotype about the dowdy librarian who gets set free sexually by the mystery male who somehow knows he's latched on to the one hottie card-catalogette in town who's wearing a thong and bustier under her gray, frumpy suit.

Personally, I always thought the skank librarian was more likely. Scary, but likely."

She ground her teeth. "Actually, I fall under the only heading of librarian I know. Hard-working, sincere, interested, capable—"

His wink stopped her. "I'm just playing around with you."

Skank librarian, indeed. She thought about her sister and her sister's reputation, which was nonexistent now. It was up to her to set a good example and to be the most upright Cakes she could be.

"I shouldn't be playing around with you, probably," he said. "You broke your bed. You might be dangerous." He pulled a huge jackknife from his pocket and began marking off sections on the wood.

"Oh, yeah." Nina sank onto a chair. "You're in big danger from me."

"Well, there's danger. And then there's *danger*. That's what I always say."

"Profound."

He glanced up at her. "Yeah. Maybe not by a librarian's standards. But it works for me."

She sighed. "So, I guess you wouldn't be

brandishing a knife that big if you didn't want it commented on."

He gave her a devilish wink. "I'm not packing small anything, peachy."

She rolled her eyes. "Of course not."

"So, tell me about your sister."

"No."

He marked some notches. "Okay."

"Tell me about your brother who wears the hat on his face."

"Why? You dig him?"

She laughed. "Dig? How can I dig a guy whose face I haven't seen?"

He looked at her, his eyes full of mischief. She wondered about that face and those eyes. What would she read in those eyes if she and he were alone together on a moonlit night—

"Maybe a face isn't what's important about a man."

She raised her brows. "Then what is?"

He stuck his knife in the floor and lifted a handsaw to the wood. "The size of his… knife." The look on her face made him laugh. "Fooled ya. You thought I was going to say something else."

"I did not!"

"Whatever."

"I won't bother to return fire. But I could, with everything I've heard about cowboys since I've been here."

"Hardworking, sincere, interested, capable—"

"That's not what my sister would say," Nina said. "She would probably say loose, loser, dishonest and wish-I'd-never-met-him."

"Hey, that's my bro—"

She stared at him. "Yes? Your what?"

He shook his head. "This is all wrong."

"Why?"

"Because." He stood, looking at her thoughtfully. "My name is Navarro Jefferson."

Her heart started a slow thud. "Jefferson?"

"Jefferson. I'm Last's older brother."

"I see." She backed away from him, turning her face. "Thank you for carrying up the lumber," she said pointedly. "You can go now."

"I could, but I think you've marked this wrong," he said, kneeling to look at the pencil markings on the slat. "What happened to this bed, anyway? You got splinters in the drapes."

She didn't want to think about what had happened to her charmed bed, especially since she suspected its shattered slats might have been Last Jefferson's doing. Her stomach churned. And now she had one of the infamous Jefferson brothers alone in the room with her and her broken bed.

He had been deceiving her by not telling her immediately that he was a Jefferson. For a minute she had nearly been taken in by that not-so-suave, good-ol-cowboy facade.

Whew. Close call.

"Hey," Navarro said. "I am sorry about your sister. We'll get to the bottom of matters. I promise."

Still not facing him, and blinking away tears, Nina shook her head. It didn't matter now. Not really. All her sister's dreams for the new life she'd hoped to find in Texas were as shattered as the bed. By a Jefferson cowboy. Now, Nina's goal was to put the bed back together and to recapture the charm.

One day she was going to need that charm for herself.

Chapter Two

So much for the peach being a possibility. Navarro glanced over at Nina, who was studiously ignoring him. That was his invitation to leave, but perversely, he wanted to stay.

It was her roundness, he decided, that he found so delicious. He wanted to take a bite of her—bad. "So, maybe we'll have to agree to work together."

She turned to face him. "What do you mean?"

He shrugged. "You're not happy. We're not happy. No one's exactly thrilled about the situation. Valentine's suing us, you know."

"She has a right to financial assistance from the father of her child."

"Maybe. If Last is the father."

Nina gasped. "How dare you?"

"Hold on there, sparky. We have a right to wonder. Last only saw her one night."

"Okay." Nina crossed her arms. "How is saying something like that helping us to work together?"

He scratched his head for a minute, thinking hard. Crockett would handle this moment so much better; he'd just sweep Nina into bed and somehow the problem would solve itself.

No, that thought didn't make Navarro feel better.

Well, if he was their oldest brother, he'd find some anal-retentive solution to talking Nina down out of her tree.

Or maybe not. Mason had never figured out their next-door neighbor and family friend, Mimi, so it was no use looking to his brother's example for inspiration.

Nor Last's. The brother with the lollipop-colored memories of the way their family used to be had kept the brothers hewn to hearth and home to make him happy. Until this latest escapade.

Crockett maybe? Archer? Bandera?

No, no and no.

It was up to him to sort out this huge problem. He could wind up a hero, if he figured out a way to fix it. The family could get back to its version of normal, if he played his cards right.

"Hey," he said, his voice calm, the way it would sound if he was soothing a skittish mare. "Let's get back to fixing this bed. Then we'll talk about the other."

That would give him time to think.

"Actually, I feel very awkward having you help me," Nina said. "It feels wrong."

"You don't owe me anything—"

"I'm not suggesting that I do," she snapped. "More like you owe us."

Navarro cautioned himself to keep his cool. He upgraded her from snippy little peach to fiery. Gently he began sawing at a piece of lumber, keeping straight to the line he'd marked with his knife. "So, this bed means a lot to you."

"Yes. I'm going to get pregnant in it one day."

He miscued the saw and went into the hardwood floor. "Damn!" Checking the damage, he said, "We'll pull the rug over that when I'm finished."

"It doesn't matter," she said, sitting on the floor. "We're already being charged damages for the room."

"Really? By whom?"

"Marvella. When the bed broke, it scratched up the floor."

He glanced under what remained of the frame. "Does seem as if she has a point. So, are…you planning on getting pregnant soon?"

"First, I'd have to find the man, wouldn't I?" She gave him a pointed look. "And I haven't met the right one yet."

"Every day brings a new opportunity," he said cheerfully.

"Thank you for your opinion, which was unsolicited, I believe."

He grinned, relieved that there was no boyfriend hanging around her. "So, what if your husband of choice doesn't want kids? I, myself, for example, do not want children. Nor marriage, but that sort of goes with the territory."

"Then he wouldn't be the right man, would he?"

"Now that was a very sensible, librarian-style answer," Navarro said approvingly.

"No messing about. No worrying about broken hearts. Just, when I meet the right man, it will all happen the way I imagine it."

Her eyes narrowed. "Are you making fun of me?"

"No." He returned to sawing, waiting for her to comment further, since he'd obviously given her something to yammer back at him about.

But she sat quietly, watching him.

He kind of liked her watching him. To be honest, he liked having her full attention. "I would have thought a cute librarian like you would have already been dragged down to the secret labyrinth of the book stacks by now."

"I would slap anybody who tried," she said, her tone even.

"Oh." He made a mental note not to get slapped.

"No man with he-man tendencies would be the man for me," she told him. "I like gentlemen."

Uh-oh. No one was ever going to accuse any of the Jeffersons of being gentle. "So, how did you say this bed ended up in this pitiful condition?"

"Best as I can tell, it happened the night your brother was here."

He stopped what he was doing and gave her his full attention. "Last would not break a lady's bed and then leave her to deal with the consequences of having no place to sleep."

"Please."

"You don't know my brother."

"I don't have to. I've seen all I need to."

Navarro had to admit his patience was starting to slide out the window. It was a cursed thing, Jefferson patience. Very rare, very mercurial and, sometimes, very hard to keep under one's hat. "Did your sister say that Last was responsible?"

"I think she felt that accusing him of the baby matter was sufficient. I, however, feel that he should be held accountable for everything he's done."

Okay. Navarro realized that facts had to be faced. He was in a room, developing hots for the only woman on the planet who seemed to be secretly designed as his nemesis. There was no happy meeting point between them; there would be no sweet build up to the happy climax. "Moving on," he said. "This should be fairly easy to finish."

"Good."

He ground his teeth at the "And well it should!" tone. It so reminded him of being in the library with old Mrs. Farklewell. Every time the Jefferson boys were in the school library, they heard a constant litany of "Shh! Shh!" in the tone that only a first-chair violinist and a librarian could muster.

"Well, look who we have here!"

Navarro glanced up at the woman in the doorway. She wore a lot of makeup and seemed very pleased to see him. Marvella.

"A Jefferson." She fairly crowed. "Cleaning up the mess baby brother left behind."

The hair under Navarro's hat started itching. "I'm cleaning up a mess. That's all I have to say."

She stroked the black kitten she held in her hands. "And getting acquainted with your future sister-in-law. How nice!"

Navarro and Nina glanced at each other.

"Family time is so important. You feel free to stay as long as you like. Which Jefferson are you, by the way?"

"Navarro, ma'am," he said automatically, the polite habit coming hard after many years of Mason knocking manners into their heads.

"Well, Navarro, there is a rodeo coming up." She smiled at him. "You know how I love those Jefferson brothers riding for my salon."

"I—"

"Someone's got to pay for this damage," she said, the expression on her face full of faux concern. "Such a shame to scar up a nice hardwood floor this way. I believe one of the screws even embedded itself in that wall," she said, pointing. "You know, Last is the first Jefferson brother who's come in here and treated my home like a shabby saloon. The rest of your brothers seem to prefer the heart-shaped spa." She shook her head. "But maybe he prefers dry land. Oh, well, no matter. I'll leave a note at the desk saying you're to have run of the house while you're here. Think about my offer."

She glided from the doorway.

Navarro turned to face Nina. The peach had gone truly pale. Putting the saw down, he sat on the floor. "Holy smokes, she's evil."

"On that, we can agree." Nina nodded at him.

"So we need to play on the same team, against her. Don't you think?"

"No."

"Why not?"

"Because that's what she's expecting. She wants you and I to band together."

"To what purpose?"

"I don't know. Maybe so you'll pay for the room damages. She can charge you more than me, obviously. Librarians don't make that much."

"So I'll pay the damages."

She looked at him, her blue eyes hopeful. "It's nice of you to offer without me having to ask you to pay for your brother's mess."

"You know," Navarro said, "it takes two people in a bed to make something happen."

"That would be the premise," she agreed. "And something happened."

"But I think your theory is too obvious," Navarro said thoughtfully, trying not to stare at her ankles as she crossed them delicately in front of her. "I think Marvella would rather see us at each other's throats. Divide and conquer."

"Elaborate, but possible," Nina said, nodding. "What would she gain?"

"Two pawns. If there are bad feelings between us, Marvella is free to work her witchery without us being the wiser."

"You may have a point," Nina said reluctantly. "In fact, it has always been the enemy's way to weaken by division, according to many of the great moments in history."

"Exactly." Navarro held out his hand. "Let's shake on working together."

"I don't know," Nina said. "We're related now, by Valentine's baby. Shaking seems quite weird."

But she put her hand in his and, later, after Navarro had time to review his actions, he would often wonder if this was the moment that changed his destiny.

He pulled Nina toward him and kissed her square on the lips.

He waited for the smacking he so righteously deserved and which she'd all but promised any man who tried to drag her into the metaphorical book stacks—but, to his amazement, Nina put her little hand behind his head and held him as she kissed him with a heated peachiness a man could only pray he experienced once in his life.

One shot. That was usually all a man ever got at something like this. Navarro was not known for wasting time or energy. Pulling Nina into his lap, he kissed her deeply, enjoying her passion and her surrender. Maybe all the more sweet because it was wrong, Navarro kissed her hard, fast, wanting as much of her as he could get.

"Ahem!"

Nina jumped out of his lap like a timed-release spring, fleeing a good yard away from him. "Damn it, Crockett!" Navarro said. "What the hell?"

"I might say the same. You were supposed to be carrying some lumber up here, bro. I thought maybe Marvella had you in her clutches."

"Not *quite*." Navarro cursed his empty lap, wanting Nina back immediately. He turned to look at Nina—who was staring at Crockett.

"Twins?" she said. "Twins?"

Crockett grinned. "Two for the price of one."

Navarro winced. "Not smooth, bro."

Crockett glanced at him. "Maybe I should start marking off some wood and keep my mouth shut."

"Excellent idea." Navarro looked at Nina, realizing unhappiness was her key emotion. "Hey," he said softly.

"No," she said automatically. She shook her head. "No."

Regret filled Navarro that the moment was lost. But it had been sweet while it lasted—and if he ever got a chance to recapture it, he was going to go for it.

Consequences be damned.

NINA COULDN'T BELIEVE her eyes. There were two versions of the man she'd just kissed putting her charmed bed back together! The only way she could tell them apart right now was by shirt color. And personality. Crockett was the brash, outspoken one. Navarro was a methodical thinker. Which should make him boring—

but he wasn't. Her lips were still on fire from his kiss!

How embarrassing to plant herself in his lap—despite all her good intentions to the contrary! Maybe that was part of his plan, to show that neither of the Cakes sisters could be counted on not to fall under a man's spell of temptation.

She stared at the brothers' industriously bent heads and decided that probably wasn't the case. They seemed more hot-blooded than deceptive. *Although I wouldn't count out the deceptive part, either.*

Okay, she just had to never lose her mind around Navarro again. And then everything would be fine.

"Friends?" he asked her.

"I'm not sure," she replied.

"I'm voting for kissing cousins," Crockett said with a grin. "Now that we're all related, anyway."

Navarro slapped him upside the head. Nina smiled. "We're not related yet," she told him.

"We're related to Valentine's baby," Crockett replied. "And anyway, once you've kissed a Jefferson, you'll never be able to—ow!" He pulled back from his brother's slap. "It's true, all the women say it!"

"Say what?" Nina asked.

"Nothing," Navarro said.

"No, tell me. I want to know."

Navarro sighed. "The saying goes that 'Once you've kissed a Jefferson man, you'll kiss anything he wants you to.'"

Nina laughed out loud. "Is that a saying you brothers made up? To create your own mystique?"

Navarro shrugged.

Crockett shook his head solemnly. "We've never had to toot our own horns."

"Oh, brother." Nina stared out the window. "Hey, look!"

The brothers came to stand beside her to stare down into the courtyard. Marvella was talking to Valentine, who appeared to be upset.

"I'm going down there," Nina said, but Navarro held her back.

"Hold on," he said. "Let's be good spies."

"My sister needs me!"

"No. She needs something, but not necessarily you butting into her business."

She pulled herself out of his hands. "Since when did you become my guardian?" she demanded, keeping a watch on Valentine who was now wiping at her eyes.

"Tried to tell you," Crockett said. "Once you've kissed one of us, you'll never want to let go of him."

"That's not what you said," Nina said, outraged.

"I'm paraphrasing." Crockett shrugged. "Most women in your position would be happy right now."

"My position? What position is that?"

Crockett never took his eyes off Valentine. Nina had a feeling he was talking by rote, ladling the same ol' bunch of nonsense the brothers probably gave every woman.

"Me and Navarro and a pretty bed all in a room with you. Most women would be happy. They might even try to fulfill some kind of twin fantasy."

Nina gasped, and Navarro put his hand over her mouth. Her eyes widened at the feel of his arm around her shoulders, his hard length lined up against her back.

"Shh," he told her. "Let Crockett think."

"Let him think!" she said, pulling free. "All he does is…is talk about *sex*."

Navarro nodded. "That's what a man does when he's thinking. But trust me, there's some serious busywork going on under that hat."

"I need to be with my sister," Nina said.

"No," Crockett said, waving her back.

"You don't care what happens to her! You don't care that she's upset!"

"Sure we do," Navarro said. "She might be carrying Jefferson goods."

Nina whipped around to stare into Navarro's eyes. *"Goods?"*

"Okay," Crockett said. "Here's the deal. Marvella wants Valentine to do something she doesn't want to. Valentine is upset. I'm going to nonchalantly stroll outside for a smoke."

"You don't smoke," Navarro said.

"Sure I do, for this charade. And Marvella's going to think I'm you," he told Navarro. "So don't blow my cover by letting her know there's two of us in the house."

"What do you want me to do?"

"Keep your eye on the peach. But don't do anything else, because I might need a rescue. Listen in case I shout."

"What's the point to this?" Nina asked.

"Nemo salis satis sapit," Crockett said, heading out the door.

"What?" Nina said. "What did he just mumble?"

"Two heads are better than one, loosely translated," Navarro said, leaning so he could spy from behind the curtain more easily. "Sometimes Crockett likes Latin. As do I."

"You guys are really weird," Nina said. "I don't know if having two heads is a plus for you."

"But you liked kissing me. Admit it," he said, staring down as his brother entered the courtyard, whistling innocently.

"Would you stop?" Nina demanded. "That's exactly what your brother did. Talk about meaningful things while your mind is on something else."

"We have excellent focus," Navarro said. "And we've been good way too long."

"Whatever." Nina watched Marvella

greet Crockett. "Think she'll notice he has on a different shirt?"

"No. No one gets past the pretty face."

Nina rolled her eyes.

"Besides, he'd just say he changed, and Marvella wouldn't doubt that because a cowboy always carries a change."

"I wonder why," Nina said dryly.

"Hey, we're trying to help you here, if you hadn't noticed."

"What's Latin for 'I'm not exactly buying that'?"

He ran a finger slowly up the back of her neck and Nina shivered. "So tell me again about how much you liked kissing me."

"I grade your ego an A-plus," Nina murmured. "But clearly it was you who liked kissing me since you can't stop talking about it."

Outside, Crockett plucked a rose and handed it to Marvella, which she took with a laugh. To the casual bystander, it would appear to be any other Sunday afternoon, passed pleasantly by people who enjoyed each other's company.

Only the flash of Valentine's face as she

glanced up at Nina's window gave away the mirage.

"Something's not right," Nina murmured.

"I know. We're going to help you fix it. You're new to town. We have to spot you some lag time on learning how to outwit Marvella."

"But that's my sister!"

"It's okay," Navarro said. "Trust me." Then he made her shiver again as he put an arm around her. "So back to the kiss we shared—"

"A mistake of epic proportions."

"Really?" He turned to face her.

"Yes."

"So you'll not be kissing anything of mine I ask—"

"No."

He raised his brows. "Well, that is new."

"You're not fooling me, Navarro Jefferson. Any woman with an ounce of sanity would listen to the bull you're peddling and say, 'No, thank you.'"

"I like your sense of self-respect." He turned her head gently so she was looking down into the courtyard again. "Now watch Crockett close the deal."

Nina watched, amazed, as Crockett led Valentine away from Marvella, apparently with Marvella's approval. He handed Valentine a hanky out of his pocket, which she gratefully took.

Two minutes later Crockett and Valentine walked into the bedroom.

"Are you all right?" Nina asked, rushing over to her baby sister.

"I'm fine." Valentine sank into the only chair in the room, while everyone else gathered around her. "And don't ask me to talk about it, because I can't."

"Why not?" Nina demanded.

"I just can't." Valentine turned sad eyes on Crockett. "Thanks for coming to my rescue."

"I like gratitude in a woman," Crockett said. "Maybe we should try for a foursome."

To Nina's surprise, Valentine giggled. "Pass. One Jefferson was all I needed."

"See?" Crockett said to Nina.

"Okay. Hold on a minute here," Nina said. "Everybody hear the new rule. No more joking about sexual matters. It's in very poor taste, considering the...situation."

Valentine and the two men stared at her.

"Whew, that's the librarian in her coming out," Navarro said. "No sense of humor. Where's your bun?"

Nina swept a hand over her chin-length hair. "Buns are passé for librarians. Why are you all taking this so lightly?"

"So we don't cry?" Valentine said. "Personally, I prefer their way of talking about it to yours, Nina. No offense or anything. But ever since you got here, you've been acting like I should be trundled off to a nunnery, and you're starting to make me nervous."

"Nervous?" Nina glanced at Navarro.

"There's a good chance you're repressed," he told her.

"I'm just a woman trying to take care of her family," Nina said sternly. "I take care of my family differently than you take care of yours. Certain matters deserve respect, and pregnancy is one of them."

"Yes, but I swear I've developed a twitch since you arrived," Valentine said. "Nina,

I'm never going to be able to live up to your standards."

"Ah," Navarro said. "Now we're getting to the deep issues."

"What are you talking about?" Nina said. "We're sisters. We have no deep issues to overcome."

"Yes, we do," Valentine said. "Even though I love you. Can I have a glass of water? I'm not feeling too well."

"I'll get it." Crockett sprang to do her bidding.

Navarro pulled Nina into the circle of his arms. "Don't worry," he said. "Everything is going to be fine."

"Nothing is going to be fine!" she insisted, but she didn't try to pull away. "My sister is unmarried and pregnant, and our heirloom bed is broken. How is everything going to be fine?"

"Because," Navarro said, putting his lips against her temple, "I've decided you need me."

Valentine laughed.

Nina bristled. "I have never needed anything less."

"That's not what you were saying when we kissed."

"You kissed him?" Valentine asked. "You know what that means, don't you?"

"I know, I know. It means that, in the future, I'll kiss anything he wants me to."

Valentine frowned. "No, Nina. It means that he'll love you and leave you."

Nina's skin turned cold. "He can't love me and leave me. We will never have those feelings for each other. In fact, the only reason we'll ever be on speaking terms is because of the baby."

But Nina felt another chill hit her—and she realized that she actually did like the big cowboy holding her close to his warm, strong body.

Very unlibrarianlike to fall for a man she'd only just met, especially a man who was used to women kissing him "wherever he liked." Probably running after him as though he were some kind of prince. In this part of the world, he was likely considered a great catch.

Not by me, Nina thought. *I always said*

I was going to wait for the right man to come along, and Navarro is not the man for my charmed bed!

Chapter Three

"I know what you're thinking," Navarro told Nina. "You're thinking I'm not the right man. But I am. And I'll show you. Let's get back to finishing up this bed while the girls hen-talk," he told his brother.

Nina glanced at Valentine. "Hen-talk, indeed. Could you live with that much chauvinism in your life?"

Valentine smiled. "Yes."

"How? I've worked hard to get an education and to earn respect at my job. No man's going to refer to me as a hen," Nina said to Valentine, but she was looking at Navarro.

"Mad as a wet hen," Crockett pointed out.

"As a counterpoint, I would just like

to say that I've worked hard to be a good cowboy and to earn respect at my job. Nobody is ever going to hen*peck* me," Navarro said to Crockett, but he was looking at Nina.

Valentine sighed. "Crockett says they're going to take care of me. Is that all right, Nina? I like the sound of it. I think I'm gonna go for it. I'm ready to leave the shelter of your wings."

"Again?" Nina's heart burned.

"Yes. You don't mean to, but you make me feel bad. I know I should be ashamed, but what happened has happened, and I'd rather the Jeffersons take care of me than Marvella. Or you. You need to go back to Delaware, to your life. It's too cold for me up there, and besides, I like rural life in Texas." Valentine smiled at the brothers.

"What about the lawsuit?" Nina asked.

"We're going to have to figure that out," Valentine replied. "But Crockett says he's going to help me."

"Since when did you become Rescue Ranger?" Nina demanded.

"She's reasonable," Crockett said. "Reasonable is easy to work with. We're all going to be one big happy family, anyway. Emphasis on happy."

"Told you Crockett could make matters work," Navarro said. "Henny-penny, the sky is *not* falling."

"Good one," Crockett said. "Very hen-dustrious of you to think of a famous hen."

"Yeah?" Nina looked at Navarro. "So if Crockett's so skillful, how come he didn't come to my room to fix the bed, instead of you?"

"Probably because I liked your little voice challenging me," Navarro said. "And Crockett never has been much for snippy. Too chauvinistic to stand it. I, on the other hand, am not bothered by ruffled feathers and a sharp beaking." He grinned. "Now, back to the bed." Glancing over it, he said, "So, Valentine, do you know how this bed ended up in this condition?"

Everyone stopped moving.

"Dude," Crockett began.

"Er—" Nina said, wondering why Navarro was trying to embarrass her sister.

"Last jumped on it," Valentine said. "Jumped a lot. Apparently he likes to jump on beds. I sort of thought it was freedom of expression, cowboy style."

Navarro and Crockett stared at her.

"Our little brother was jumping on your bed, hard enough to break it?" Crockett asked.

"He was having a great time," Valentine said. "I stood right over there and watched."

"That doesn't sound kinky at all," Navarro said. "I'm almost disappointed."

"Well, you have to understand the age of this bed," Valentine said. "It's an heirloom."

"Right. The heirloom charmed bed. Guaranteed potency."

"Exactly," Valentine said. "Now you just need to put it back together so it can work for Nina. She wants a baby, you know. And she's no spring chicken."

"I thought she was pushing the dark side of thirty," Navarro said. "Though she kisses like a baby."

"A baby!" Nina was outraged.

"Yeah. All sweet and tender and trusting."

She stared at him. "You, sir, are no gentleman."

He snapped his fingers. "I don't meet those librarian prerequisites. Damn."

Crockett laughed. "She wants gentle. He comes from a long line of men who know how to kiss women off their feet and enslave them with passion." Reaching over, he patted Valentine's tummy. "I can't wait to be an uncle. We're going to name him Eustus."

"No we're not," Valentine said. "We're going to name her Mary. No more Valentines and Eugenias, though those are very fine names."

Nina gasped. "No family names?"

"No." Valentine shook her head decisively. "I'm going alone on this one."

"I still don't understand why you called off the lawsuit you filed against Last," Nina said. "I came down here to help save you from the bad guys."

"Turns out they're kind of sweet," Valentine said. "Look, Nina. I'm not like you. I'm not a card-carrying feminist. I'm not looking to be the woman who has it all. I just want a man and a baby. I don't have the man, but I have the baby, and Crockett says the Jeffersons will make me part of the family. That's all I want. It replaces what you and I lost when our parents died."

"And you believe him?" Nina didn't think she could part with her trust that easily.

"Yeah. I do. Besides, the lawsuit was Marvella's idea."

The three of them stared at Valentine.

"How's that?" Navarro asked. "You mean, you girls weren't looking to free-load off some wealthy cowboys?"

Nina gave him the evil eye. "Tell me again how these men are the most gentlemanly men you'll ever meet?"

"You have a bit o' the pit in you, my peach," Navarro said. "Were you not involved in the lawsuit idea?"

"I was not," Nina said between gritted teeth. "I came down here to help my sister with her pregnancy. And to assist her in any other way possible. You know, since I've met you this afternoon," she said to Navarro, "it seems like an awful lot has changed very fast."

"We aim to please," Crockett said.

"But hold on a minute here," Nina said. "You've charmed your way into Marvella's good graces. You've talked my sister out of a lawsuit to protect her child, with nothing more than promises on your part, and—"

"And I've kissed you," Navarro said cheerfully. "All in all, a very profitable afternoon."

"You've seduced us," Nina said with a flash of understanding.

"Not yet." Navarro looked at her. "Could we count it as something you'd consider?"

Crockett grinned. "Back to that twin fantasy—"

"No!" Nina glared at both of them, completely aware they were yanking her chain. "Let's just get the bed fixed. Then we'll figure out everything else."

THREE HOURS LATER, the bed was good as new, maybe better. Valentine was completely worn out, so she lay on it, just for a test, she said, and went out like a light.

Nina said she'd better make certain the bed would hold two bodies, and she got on the bed, next to her sister. With the twilight-fresh breeze blowing warmly through the room, Nina fell asleep next to her sister.

Really annoying, especially when Navarro thought Nina should be so entranced by him that she would stay awake.

The other problem, Navarro thought as he looked at the newly refurbished bed, was that Nina was so darn upright. She really needed to loosen that librarian corset of hers. It was so tight she didn't have any fun! And he couldn't figure out how to make her take another walk on the wild side. There was every possibility he might not ever get another kiss out of her.

He needed to shake something up between them.

Maybe that's what Last had been doing when he'd jumped on the bed. Shaking things up a bit.

Then there was Crockett, who'd made himself right at home between the two napping sisters.

The dawg.

"Hey," he said, poking Crockett, who looked about as happy as any man in a nonconjugal, reclined position could be. "Wake up."

"Don' wanna," Crockett said. "I'm be-tween two women. Life is good."

"They're just sleeping," Navarro said. "And you're barely touching them."

"The future holds the key," Crockett said sleepily. "One hates to second-guess surprise and random good luck. Besides, they counterbalance the bed perfectly. Go away."

Navarro decided the handiwork they'd put into sawing and remounting the slats must have worked if it held three bodies comfortably. *Three and a half.*

"When are we leaving?" he asked. "I'm getting twitchy." Super-twitchy, watching his brother snooze so happily next to Nina. Though for the life of him, he wasn't sure why he should care.

Because when she kissed me, she lit my fire.

"I'm in no hurry," Crockett said. "Go on before you wake up my girls."

"Whatever. Call the cell when we decide on the next course of action."

He started to leave the room. Nina popped up. "I'll go with you," she said. "I'm hungry."

"That's better," he said happily.

"Not for me," Crockett complained. "Get out before you wake the other one. She needs her rest."

Nina hesitated, wondering if she should leave her sister alone in bed with a stranger. A Jefferson. Her reputation might suffer.

"Crap," Crockett said, easing up from the bed. "I knew it was too good to be true. I'll sit over here by the window. Leave the door open so we can air out and keep our reputations unscathed."

"Thanks, Crockett," Nina said gratefully.

"No prob. I'm gonna grab a quick beer out of the fridge before I take up duty. Marvella said to help myself."

"That's sort of scary," Navarro said. "But we won't think about that right now. Just one beer, okay? And I'll bring you and Sleeping Beauty a snack. Or call if she wakes up soon, and we'll come by and pick you up. We need to make plans for the future."

Crockett touched Valentine's toes on his way past the bed. She didn't move. "Out like a light," he said. "Can't get into any mischief when you're lying in bed."

"You can in *that* bed," Navarro said. "Don't even get me started on that."

"You're just mad 'cause you didn't get a turn at snuggling."

Navarro watched Nina's roundly plump posterior move down the hall in front of him. "They say that twins can read each other's minds. Do you know what I'm thinking?"

"Shut the hell up?"

"Exactly," Navarro said.

"WHAT DO YOU WANT to eat?" Navarro asked Nina once they were outside.

"We can walk to the cafeteria, or we can eat spaghetti in Marvella's kitchen. Those are the choices," she told him. "Actually, I'm not as hungry as I thought I was."

"Check it out," Navarro said. "There's Marvella's sister, Delilah."

"And Marvella." Nina watched the two women see each other on opposite sidewalks then ignore each other and turn to go into their separate salons. "Ouch," she said.

"I never want that to happen to me and Valentine. I want us to always be friends."

"Something went very wrong there. I don't think they're ever going to make up." Navarro pulled her away from the street so they could walk down the sidewalk. "You know, one thing worries me about your sister. Maybe she has a rescue-me syndrome going on."

Nina stopped. "What are you talking about?"

"She doesn't have your goals or your drive. She's content to have people take care of her."

"That doesn't make her a bad person," Nina said. "Just young and somewhat immature. And maybe it's not altogether weird, when you consider that our parents died when she was young."

"How come you're so different?"

"Because I had to be. And then because I wanted to be. I was the eldest. It's just different."

"Don't blow a geyser here, but what if Valentine got pregnant just so that someone—Last, at that moment—would have to take care of her?"

The same thought had occurred to Nina, but she didn't appreciate Navarro broaching it. "Then we'd have to accept that about her. I'm not saying she's perfect, Navarro."

"No one is." They rounded a corner on the way to the cafeteria. "It just worries me, is all. Now that she's going to have to be the protector, instead of the protected."

"What are you saying? That my sister won't make a good mother?"

"No, I'm not saying that. It's just sort of a feeling I have. Sort of a 'hey, grow up and think things through' feeling."

"What do you want her to do, Navarro?"

"Mainly take care of herself and the baby. But I'd also like to see her take more initiative with her life. Did you notice how quickly she gave up the lawsuit? That was a lot of money she was pressing us for."

"Yes, but she said it was Marvella's idea."

"And how do you think Marvella's going to react when she finds out the lawsuit is off? Especially if she was trying to squeeze my family for money by manipulating Valentine? And isn't it funny how nice Marvella's been to us since we got here. 'Have a beer…make yourself at home…ride in the rodeo for me—'"

"Apparently that's Marvella's game. Be very nice and get what you want." Nina looked at Navarro's broad shoulders and then his chest, self-consciously enjoying the view. He was a very handsome man, even if he wasn't making sense.

Navarro sighed. "She didn't expect Valentine to tell us that she was behind the lawsuit. Which follows, because I don't think Valentine could have come up with the idea by herself, and for such a heinous amount to boot. We thought we were going to have to sell the ranch. Or part of it, anyway."

"What if Marvella doesn't let Valentine terminate the lawsuit?" Nina asked, feeling somewhat ill.

"She can't stop her, but I am thinking Marvella will be plenty unhappy. That was so much money, there's no way she's not going to feel cheated." Navarro looked thoughtful. "We need a good plan. Unfortunately, I can't plan and look at your mouth. It makes me crazy."

"Does it really?" Nina asked.

"Really, really crazy. All I want to do is kiss you again. You know, you surprised me, crawling up in my lap like that. I was expecting a slap."

"Maybe next time."

"I was wondering…" Navarro said. "Is there anything between you and me besides bad feelings and some lust?"

"Lust?" Nina bent to adjust her sandal strap, then rose to meet Navarro's eyes. "Once again we have a decided difference in terms. I just wanted to kiss you. That's all it was."

His eyes widened. "Knife through my heart."

"Really." She went ahead of him on the sidewalk.

"Nina."

She turned around and faced him, her hands on her hips. "What, cowboy?"

He hesitated a moment, so she took the time to look into his eyes. Those eyes could make a less respectable woman toss her panties to the four corners of the earth.

"There was something—" he said.

"Maybe good. Maybe bad. But *was*." Her eyes softened. "I'm in a bad spot right now, Navarro. I can't help seeing what has happened to my sister. You and I have to get along, but—"

"Shh!" He pulled her to the side of the building. "Here comes someone."

"So? People come by here all the time." She tried to pull away until she heard a woman's voice.

Marvella.

Navarro's arms tensed around her. Nina fought the feeling of attraction so she could focus on eavesdropping.

"It's simple," Marvella told one of her employees. "They're going to ride for the team I sponsor. They'll have to, if they want to spring Valentine from her contract with me. Obviously the first thing they're going to do is talk her out of the lawsuit. Which is fine, because I never figured I'd get that much money out of them. I'll agree to be pleasant about the lawsuit, if they both agree to ride for me. Imagine that," Marvella said with satisfaction. "Twin Jefferson brothers. Two rides for the price of one admission ticket. It'll be like a circus attraction. And girls will come from everywhere, buying up tickets and memorabilia. My secret potion will sell like there's no tomorrow. And girls will bring the boys running," she said. Her companion laughed as they went inside the cafeteria.

"Okay, now I intensely dislike her," Nina said. "Manipulating your family was her idea all along. Valentine's such a wimp, although I hate to say it. She's got to grow a spine. You know, I really want to see her become a vertebrate."

"Hey!" He turned her to face him. "Be nice to your sis."

"I always am. But Marvella was going to gouge you by using Valentine, and Valentine should have stood up and said, 'No, thanks—have a party without me.'"

"She's pregnant," Navarro reminded her. "We Jeffersons do have some responsibility here."

She looked at him.

"I mean, I'm not exactly trying to be all honorable or anything," Navarro said. "I'd be lying if I said I wasn't trying to look good to you. We're going to be related, I guess, by baby. So," he said with a shrug, "I'll probably see you every Thanksgiving or so. Maybe at Christmas I can catch you under the mistletoe."

"Well, you're being more honest than me." She looked down the street. "Let's go before we run into Marvella. I need to ponder Valentine's next action. And mine."

He pulled her to him so that he could lift her chin and look into her eyes. "You're not listening to me. You're making me want to read a new kind of book."

"I've had enough of reading," she said, knowing he wasn't talking about books at all. "For now, I've got to think. And the first thing that comes to mind is getting Valentine away from Marvella."

"So you two should come to the ranch."

She stared at him. "Ranch?"

"Union Junction Ranch—Malfunction Junction. You'll be safe there with my family. And we can plot our course."

"What do you think Last would say about that?"

Navarro shrugged. "Whether he likes it or not, we're one big happy family. Provided, of course, that the baby is Last's. And I don't say that to be mean, but—"

"Valentine says it is."

He nodded. "Come to the ranch with me. Tonight. We'll leave Marvella a congenial kiss-my-grits note. Very congenial, for the sake of future relations. Namely, coming back to get your charmed bed."

She shook her head. "I don't want to go to the ranch. I want to live my own life. Actually, I wouldn't be averse to Valentine letting me raise her baby back in Delaware."

"What?"

She could tell that thought had never crossed this cowboy's mind.

"That's Jefferson flesh and blood you're talking about," he said on a growl. "Come on, Nina, don't make my head pop off my shoulders here."

"It's also Cakes flesh and blood. And I'm going to do what's best for Valentine. Maybe she doesn't want to live forever at your ranch. Perhaps it would be good for her to grow up and not always have someone rescue her. And, anyway, Last may not want her around."

"It doesn't matter what Last wants." His fingers tightened just a bit on her arms. "Nina, you moving away with the baby would be very hard on us Jeffersons. Let's smoke on this some more, okay? There's a way to work this out. We probably need a librarian in town."

She looked at him. "What town?"

"Union Junction."

"Why do I need to know that?"

"Won't you want a job?"

"I have a job in Dannon. I took vacation to come down here and help my sister fend off your brother."

"Fend off my…wait a minute. Last isn't exactly bothering your sister. She was the one seeking money from us."

"This whole business of taking Valentine to the ranch with you is just a way to get around talking about custody in the courts, isn't it?"

"Now hold on—"

"Anyway, you said yourself, Last wouldn't care if the whole problem disappeared. I *want* a child. If Valentine decides to return home to Dannon with me, I'd at least get to raise my sister's baby. I'm even prepared to get married so a court of law would look upon me as a model of stability. Which shouldn't be a problem because librarians are not exactly known to be wacky." She pulled peach lip gloss from her purse and applied it with a brush—all, he was certain, to make his blood boil.

"Although there may be *some* wacky librarians. I'm not saying there aren't," Nina continued. "But you know?" She pulled her blond hair up onto her head in a sweet rubber-banded ponytail, then put on black cat's-eye glasses that should have been awful but that looked funky and sexy as hell on her heart-shaped face. "It's just not the profession women go into for a good time. 'How's your Dewey decimal system today?' isn't a line men use."

"Oh, boy," Navarro said. "You are trouble with a capital T."

"And you can spell." She gave him a droll look and lightly tapped his arm. "I wear these to read to the children for story time. They also like the pointy black boots I wear and the red-and-white-striped socks. I dress like Mrs. Piggle-Wiggle, not that I expect you to know who that is. I suppose I should dress more like a muggle or a hobbit to keep current with the times, but I find that the younger children particularly enjoy the comfort and familiarity of a grandmotherly type reading them books."

"And do you read from an upside-down house?" Navarro murmured.

"Oh, you have read the books!"

"Well," Navarro said uncomfortably, not wanting to dim the excitement in her voice because he liked it, "I haven't read them personally. Dad used to read to us as kids, at night, to give Mom a break from taking care of us. It wasn't easy raising twelve boys, and her joy was a bubble bath at night while Dad read. But then, he tired out when…" He hesitated, thinking about the past. He and his brothers had enjoyed their childhoods, he couldn't deny that. But after their mother died, the reading—and a lot more—had stopped. "I haven't read a book in a while."

"I have a romance right here," Nina said, pulling a paperback from her purse. "If we go to the ranch I could read to you while you drive. I'm a fun reader. The kids love me."

He tried not to frown. "Romance isn't my thing."

"Romance? It's *everybody's* thing. I'll

read you one paragraph now, to see if you don't like it. How's that for a deal?"

He could feel the tips of his ears turning red. "I'd feel better if it was a Western."

"One paragraph. Sharing a book is a great way to get to know each other better." They sat on a bench down the street from the salon and cafeteria, and, in a soft, lulling voice, Nina began to read, "'When Domingo Carmichael ran from the burning building with the woman in his arms, he felt explosive heat at his back. Crying out for fear that she would be exposed to the inferno's blaze, he cradled the naked woman—'"

"Naked?" Navarro interrupted. "He ran out of a burning building with a naked woman in his arms? Guys only get that lucky in romance novels."

She gave him a narrow gaze. "Real life is stranger than fiction. Or so they say. No more interruptions, please. As I say during story time for the children, 'Let's use our best manners and be quiet as mice so everyone can hear!'"

"Yegods." But he tried not to laugh at

her sweet tone. "I get the hint. You just got my visuals arrested with the naked part."

"Of course. You're a man."

"Getting back to the burning building and the sweating hero and the naked lady—"

"'He cradled the naked woman to his chest. Finally far enough from the blaze, he laid her down near a stream. He took off his shirt and wrapped her in it. "Stay here," he told Amelie. "You're safe now. They need my help battling the blaze so it doesn't spread to the forest. I'll be back soon."' And that's the end of the prologue," Nina said. "Chapter one opens in a different place, six years later, with both of them married to other people, who, coincidentally, they are not deeply in love with. They never got over each other, but they both believe the other died."

"First of all," Navarro said, "no man lets a naked woman out of his sight."

"Well, she wasn't really naked anymore. She had on his shirt." Nina peered at the cover. "It's like a chamois color or something, but she's dressed."

"She has no undergarments on and that

alone would be enough to drive him insane. He'd never leave her. My belief is suspended. I rate that book a C."

"But he had to do the honorable thing and fight the fire before it reached the forest, Navarro. That's what makes her love him, that he would sacrifice even his lust for her for the higher good."

Navarro laughed. "And that's why I stick to Westerns. I like the reality. All that men being honorable, taking care of the world, then returning to the one good woman who loves them—it's garbage. It's just not true."

She stared at him. "What specifically are you having a problem with?"

He shrugged. "If you were naked, Nina, I would not leave you by a stream for any yahoo to stumble on and do harm to. *That's* reality."

"Oh."

In fact, the more he thought about a naked Nina in his arms as he carried her off to safety, the tighter his jeans got. He shifted surreptitiously. "It sounds like their location was pretty remote. What if there were…I don't know, wild animals around? Like crocs in the stream. Or snakes, even.

Why would he leave her when he should be protecting her? I wouldn't leave my naked woman around for the world to see. No way."

"Oh."

"You see, I'm right. Because something did happen. They didn't see each other again for six years. That means his naked lady went somewhere or got taken somewhere by someone. And he should have been there to take care of her and get her to safety. That's no hero. John Wayne wouldn't leave his naked woman lying around like an empty pack of Marlboro cigarettes."

"All right," Nina said crossly. "Enough with the manly analysis of my one-paragraph experiment. I should have known better than to expect you not to get sidetracked by the visuals."

"Well, it was a naked woman, come on already." He glanced at her. "Did you expect I'd be concentrating on the idyllic stream? Don't get mad, Nina. I am a man. Read on, if it'll make you feel better. I promise not to interrupt."

"I can't read on. I made all that up." She

snapped the paperback shut and put it in her purse.

"What do you mean?"

"I mean that I knew we couldn't share anything more than that kiss. I dream of someday having romance in my charmed bed. You claim to be a realist and a man of action. I knew you would guffaw, cheapen or otherwise submit my romantic escapism to humiliation. In order not to lose the pleasure of reading this book, I made something up to save myself." Her look was very smug. "And as we both can see, it was a very practical thing for me to do. You did, in fact, guffaw and try to cheapen the story, just because you can't handle the idea of romance as viable escapism. I own a *charmed* bed. Romance is part of my internal belief system."

"Now, look," Navarro said. "I feel the need to defend myself here. You didn't give me a hero to believe in. No man leaves his naked woman lying around. Now if you told me he'd gone commando and given her his shirt while he'd left to put out the fire—"

"What do you mean 'gone commando'?"

How much did a man have to explain to a woman? Especially one he couldn't help imagining in the buff. He'd put a bet on her bottom being as soft as rose petals. "Gone commando. Sans Calvins. His rider without a jockey."

"So you're saying that if he'd given her his underwear as well as his shirt—"

Navarro held up his hand to wave off the topic. "That would be heroic, practical and believable. Having made certain that her lily pads as well as her pussy willows were secure, he could then go battle the fire and save the world. And I'm only using those illustrations because he dumped her by a stream, so don't get all excited."

"A man can battle a blaze without underwear."

He nodded. "Certainly. But he can't leave his woman without proper covering."

"Did it ever occur to you that perhaps the heroine could take care of herself?"

"Of course," he said impatiently. "It's just that, from the romantic escapism perspective that we're discussing, the hero knows his lady can do anything. But he *chooses* to protect her modesty, which demonstrates his total concern and love for her." He glanced at her, his gaze roaming over her hotly. "It was a good attempt on your part to make a point about my lack of romance appreciation, but you'll have to concede that my way of telling the story is much more the definition of true romance."

"I never knew that a man giving a woman his underwear was considered romantic."

"They say we learn something new every day," Navarro said, happy to make his point.

"Would I be wearing briefs or boxers?"

He glanced at her. "Neither, hopefully."

"If you rescued me. Would I be wearing boxers or briefs?"

"Now that's personal." He frowned. He'd wondered whether her bras were cotton or satin, but there was no way she'd ever rescue him and loan him a brassiere, so he really couldn't segue into that question. "But today, you'd be wearing boxers with happy faces and candy canes on them."

"I'd look lovely in the jungle wearing those. Nothing like big, yellow moon faces and bright red candy canes to keep me camouflaged from the wildlife."

"Now *you* tell *me*."

"What?"

"You know, boxers or briefs kind of stuff."

"You want to know if I rescued you today and gave you my most personal article of clothing to protect your modesty, what you'd be wearing?"

Yes, yes, yes! He mentally rubbed his palms together. *What does a librarian wear to peruse the card catalog?*

"White granny panties that stretch to the third rib," Nina said.

The visuals dimmed his desire as he considered the elastic required to stretch to the third rib. *Okay,* Navarro thought, *my jeans are more comfortable.*

"No comment?" she asked. "No more questions?"

"I think I'm done," he said.

"Good." She laughed. "I have trouble seeing you in white granny panties, but it would keep you safe from the wildlife."

"I reckon. Even the crocs don't want those."

"Disappointed?"

He heard the giggle in her tone. "No."

"You were hoping I'd send you through the jungle in a lacy lavender thong."

He grunted. The thing about Nina was that she kept him pinned in every corner. "I'd stick with commando. But I'd let you give me your lavender thong and I'd keep it safe to remember you by during the six years the story said we'd be apart. Although I would never lose a woman I loved for six years. Not even for six minutes." She couldn't possibly know how personally the Jefferson men took losing their women. His father, Maverick, and Mason were prime examples of one-woman men who never recovered. Actually, their ranching neighbor, Sheriff Cannady, Mimi's father, could be counted in that category, too.

Dang, I don't want to end up a head case over a woman. This one already makes me crazy. Bad opening scene to a story, actually.

Nina didn't comment on his theory. But her face took on a considering expression. Her eyes held his and her lips trembled just a bit.

Oh, yeah, he thought. *A lacy lavender thong and man commando. We got ourselves a visual now!*

Problem was, his jeans were tight again, Nina had gone silent on him and he was taking a woman home who told her own yarns to keep her romantic illusions safe.

He sighed. "We've got trouble, Mrs. Piggle-Wiggle," he said. "You're never going to come over to my side."

"Just protecting my own, cowboy, and worrying about the burning building later."

"Girding yourself with a lavender thong."

"We're writing the hard part now," Nina said. "The real-life stuff. No happy faces and candy canes."

He shook his head. "You belong at Malfunction Junction."

She shook her head. "Don't try to seduce me. You may kiss fabulously, but now I see that anything more between us is impractical. And though I may be romantic, I have a hugely practical side."

He pulled her up from the bench. "Come on. You scared me so bad with the granny panties, I'm forced to surrender. From now on, we're just friends."

"Friendship is good," Nina said, wondering why the thought made her feel so alone.

Navarro turned to her. "I have one question."

"Okay." She met his gaze.

"What's with the granny panties-security fence you're putting up?" His gaze went from her soft, full lips to her wide eyes watching him behind her cat's-eye spectacles. "'Cause I have a funny feeling you're not being completely candid with me, Mrs. Piggle-Wiggle."

Chapter Four

Nina eyed Navarro warily. "What fence?"

"You don't really think I believe you have on white underwear up to your third rib?" He knew she was fibbing—and every good fib had a reason for a cover-up.

He was sure Nina liked secreting information; she was a good little librarian with a storehouse of the stuff. His peachy card-catalogette.

"I don't care what you believe," she said. "My underthings are none of your business."

"Yeah, but see, that's what bothers me. It *isn't* any of my business. So you go and tell me a huge whopper, which is almost shouting, 'Check me out! Catch me if you can!'" He winked at her. "And as I've told you before, snippy defiance is almost foreplay for me. By heaven, it *is* foreplay for me."

He pulled her tight against him. One kiss should do it. One kiss should be enough to get the ants out of his pants where Nina was concerned. Then he could figure out whether the first kiss had been as good as he'd thought it was—because no kiss should make a man as crazy as that kiss had made him.

Surely he'd been inside the Never Lonely Cut-n-Gurls salon too long, breathing perfume pumped through the air-conditioning system so that a man couldn't breathe without getting an itch for a woman.

But the air conditioner hadn't been on, he remembered, and Nina felt just as good in his arms this time as she had before. He was losing his mind, and worse, he was losing his grip on reality. "You're soft," he told her.

"You're really hard," she murmured between kisses. "And I don't know why I'm letting you kiss me on the street where anyone can see us."

"Because we're slaves to passion," he said, winding his fingers into her hair so that he could take down that crazy bird's-nest bun he was pretty sure she'd twisted up to annoy him. "You're sexually undiscovered, book-stacks-stalking librarian, and I'm the rowdy, irresistible cowboy with a heart of gold to whom the ladies throw lavender thongs."

Nina laughed, but he wouldn't let her pull away. So she stayed in his arms, where he wanted her.

"Your reputation is all that?" she asked.

"I'd like to shelve something of yours," he said, biting her ear gently. "And maybe catalog something." He sucked where he'd bit. "And then I'm pretty sure I'd charge you an overdue fine." He slid his hands down to her fanny, tracing along her skirt line. "Tell me you're overdue. Because I *know* I am."

She pulled away and dragged him by the hand toward Marvella's salon. "You're scaring me, cowboy. I do not want to be caught out in the jungle where there's no condom machine."

"One of us is thinking things through."

"That's me. The sensible one. Although

you nearly had me losing my sense back there."

"Well, that will have to be enough to keep me living," Navarro said, stopping suddenly about a hundred feet from the salon. "What's going on up there?"

A moving truck was outside, with two men loading up Nina's precious charmed bed.

Nina began running. "Stop! Stop!"

"Oh, man. The life of a librarian is so dull," Navarro muttered, hoofing after Nina.

The men saw her coming, shut the doors, jumped inside the truck and drove away before she could get there. "What just happened?" she demanded of Valentine, who was in the doorway, sobbing.

"Before Marvella went to lunch she said I owed her the bed since I was leaving her employment," Valentine said, "and because I told her I was backing out of the lawsuit. She sent those men to take it. I'm so sorry, Nina. I've lost your bed."

In silence, Nina stared down the street after the truck.

Navarro cleared his throat. "We'll get it back," he promised. "Somehow."

"It's a well-known antique," Nina said dully. "We had three offers on that bed, just recently. Many years ago, one of the presidents slept in that bed with his girl-friend. We don't talk about that, of course, but everyone knew about it at the time."

"Did she have a baby?" Navarro wanted to know. "Because if she did, that'd be kind of spooky." When Nina didn't reply, he sighed and turned to Valentine. "Where's my brother?"

"Sleeping off the effects of the beers he got out of the fridge," Valentine said. "That man can't hold his liquor. Which somewhat reminded me of his younger brother, but I won't mention that since making compari-sons in the family can be hard on a child's self-esteem."

He was going to ignore the barb to Last and focus on the reputational issue, Na-varro decided. "Not to brag, but all Jef-fersons can hold their liquor. Show me my twin. I'm sure he's just exhausted from the busy afternoon we've had here in Lonely Hearts Station."

He put his arms around Nina, who looked stunned, still staring after the truck. "It's going to be okay."

"How dare she?" Nina whispered.

Navarro sighed. "Marvella just does. Let's find Crockett and get out of here. Now we're definitely going to take you to the ranch."

"My poor bed," Nina moaned. "It's been through such an adventure."

"Maybe one day someone will write a book about it," Navarro said, secretly worried that Nina might not ever see her beloved bed again. "Back to the ranch to regroup. I need to touch Tara so I can think. You've read *Gone With The Wind,* haven't you?"

"My Tara's on a trip in a delivery van," Nina said sadly.

"I'll fix it," Navarro said, hoping he was right. "Nothing bad can happen to it. I promise. I'm sure Marvella can be reasoned with."

"MARVELLA CAN'T BE reasoned with," Navarro said an hour later as the four of them met at the truck. He'd tried every angle, but Marvella'd had the bases covered: Valentine's salary had been paid in advance, Marvella had fired Valentine for incompetence—with no letter of recommendation—and, as her landlord, she had a right to Valentine's possessions by law to cover expenses. Navarro had put a swift call into Mimi's husband, Brian, and discovered that Marvella was within her rights due to the signed contract.

He looked at Nina with a heavy heart. "I even offered her money. She wouldn't take it. Frankly, I think she's doing this to get to Delilah, somehow, but I can't prove it."

Nina sighed. "You tried."

Valentine sniffled. Crockett, now fully recovered, let out a curse word.

"I shouldn't have drank that beer," he said. "It knocked me on my keister."

"It was Marvella's house special," Valentine said. "I didn't notice what he'd grabbed till it was too late."

"You left me to take care of your sister," Crockett said to Nina. "I was supposed to be the keeper of the bed. And I fell asleep on the job."

"It's okay," Nina said. "At least you didn't jump on the bed and break it again."

"You only drank one. Last drank two or three or maybe four of those things," Valentine said. "He told me he could put down a six-pack and never burp."

"Well, he certainly did burp," Navarro said. "Let's go home."

Nina looked at him.

"Don't start," he said.

"I wasn't going to," she replied. "It's been a long day and all I want to do is go to sleep. Off to the ranch."

He grinned and opened the truck door. "Your chariot awaits."

Two hours later, a group of Jefferson brothers stood on the porch, staring at Valentine and Nina. Navarro had apparently called ahead and announced their imminent arrival.

Last Jefferson didn't make any attempt to hide his dismay at seeing Valentine when she got out of the truck.

"I don't understand why you brought her here," Last said to Navarro. "Are you trying to kill me?"

Nina swallowed, feeling sorry for Valentine. "Hi," she said.

No one said anything in return. The brothers stared at her.

"Navarro, dude. What were you thinking, man?" Calhoun asked. "We've got a lot on our hands. We didn't exactly need this right now."

Archer nodded. "Not to be abrupt, Ms. Nina, but I'm sure you realize that, with your sister's financial demands, we feel that our brother has made an error in bringing you here."

"Easy, boys," Navarro said. "Everything's under control."

"Clearly we have a lot to talk about," Archer said. "Why don't you come in, Nina?"

She hesitated, holding her sister's hand to comfort her. Last was staring at Valentine, his face a myriad of mixed emotions.

"Ladies," Navarro said, "don't get spooked by my brothers. They're just a bit ornery and sometimes blunt-spoken because they don't see many women. At least women they carry on a conversation with." He grimaced at Last. "Don't get on the lady's bad side. You're related to her now, dunce, so show her some respect. It's the least we can *all* do."

Nina flashed Navarro a grateful smile.

He nodded. "Can't leave you hanging bare-assed around the crocs. They have no manners whatsoever."

"What the hell are you talking about?" Calhoun demanded.

Navarro shrugged, ignoring him to motion to the women. Nina and Valentine followed as he led them toward the house.

"I can offer you sleeping accommodations here, but I think you might be happiest in what we call house number three. Or, you can go to Mimi's, next door. Mimi's like our little sister, only more hellish. We love her dearly. She's got a new baby, and you could get some practice holding her for when you'll be an auntie."

"Why are you suddenly being so easygoing about this?" Nina asked.

He frowned. "I should have explained. Townsfolk call our ranch Malfunction Junction for a reason. We don't function well. My brothers have few manners and they're hard to get along with in just about every situation. But I'm not going to leave you stranded."

Her heart beat a little faster. He was good with the ladies, she reminded herself. It meant nothing that he was protecting her and her sister from his brothers.

It was all about the baby.

Navarro smiled at her reassuringly and Nina felt stirrings for him that she didn't want to feel. It was a doomed emotion, and she recognized that.

"Where did you find her, is what I want to know," Last asked, coming up behind them. "Not to be rude, but how did you end up bringing Valentine's sister home?"

"It was a funny thing. She was looking for someone to carry some lumber to fix their bed. There I was."

"There you were," Last repeated. "What were you doing in Lonely Hearts Station?"

"He was trying to spy on my sister." Nina gave Navarro a triumphant smile. "Not that it did any good."

Last shook his head.

"It's nice to finally meet you," Nina said.

Last couldn't meet her gaze. "I wish I could say the same. I'm not trying to sound unfriendly, it's just that we as family tend to overhelp each other. It doesn't always turn out right."

"I understand." She sent a glance to Navarro. "Too many crocs in the kitchen."

Navarro held up a hand. "Hey, I was simply looking for the refrigerator."

A car horn blaring made them all turn.

"Who is that?" Archer demanded. "Driving like a maniac?"

A powder-blue VW Bug drove up the ranch road, bumping and bouncing as a man waved his hat out the driver's side window.

"If that's not the silliest thing I ever saw," Calhoun said. "Somebody tell the lil' Bug not to hurt itself getting to the ranch. We'll be picking parts out of the road for days."

"That's Doc, the crazy son of a mouse," Bandera said. "What's he driving?"

"I called him before we left Lonely Hearts Station," Navarro said. "I want him to meet Valentine."

Nina glanced at him with surprise. He really *was* all about the pregnancy. The VW horn beep-beep-beeped merrily as it rumbled toward them, a round harbinger of the moment they would all soon be facing. Last made a sound of disgust and left the gathering.

"While he's here, he can examine Crockett, who's still in the truck with a headache and a hangover. Though I doubt there's much he can do. I could use some romantic escapism right about now," Navarro said to Nina. "Relational issues are always so wearing in families. And now ours is growing. I feel so ganged-up-on."

She gave him wide eyes. "*'Et tu, Brute?'*"

He sighed. "Caesar wasn't exactly escapism."

The doctor got out of the car, his white hair gleaming in the sun. "Howdy, boys," he said.

"Howdy, Doc Gonzalez," they chorused.

"And two pretty ladies," he said with a grin. "The Jefferson boys, ugly goats that they are, always manage to find nice women to put up with them."

Nina grinned at Navarro. "Well, maybe this is the part of the story where everything is fun."

Navarro looked at her, his brows raised.

"Nina, what are you talking about?" Valentine asked.

"Just that there are a lot of stories being told. Navarro, wouldn't you love to invite us in so we don't stand out here all day like a circus without a ringleader?"

"Yegods, she has a sharp tongue on her," Calhoun whispered.

"Yeah, but I like her sense of direction. She always seems to know where I should be going, and it's usually someplace I didn't expect. It's kind of exciting," Navarro said with a grin.

"Whatever," Calhoun said under his breath. "Are you really inviting Last's floozy into the house so she can scope out what we've got?"

"Which is, as far as I can determine," Navarro said loud enough for Nina to hear, "not a damn thing more or less than we're ever going to have. We have a baby to talk about, so, awkward as this may be, we need to head indoors and pour ourselves a cold one. Lemonade, that is, since we're having a baby. Archer, you fix us up. C'mon, Doc. Thanks for coming out."

Everyone waited, paralyzed by Valentine's presence in their midst. Valentine clutched Nina's hand, and Nina ached for her. "Come on," she told her sister. "I'm listening to Navarro. He knows all about rescues." She gave him an airy nod as she walked past him to go up the steps. "Thank you," she said over her shoulder.

"You're welcome," he said. "I'm gonna keep close to you, though. There's no telling what you might have up your sleeve."

"Could be dangerous," she told him.

"Could be."

"Is there something going on between you two that I should know about?" Valentine asked as Nina dragged her sister forward. "Because you seem to have a certain repartee usually reserved for couples who—"

"No," Nina said with finality. "We have no certain repartee."

"None at all," Navarro said cheerfully.

Chapter Five

The family gathered in the kitchen, an awkward conglomeration of people who knew they had to talk but didn't really want to. Two dozen cupcakes, fresh from the Union Junction cafeteria, lay in the center of the table, untouched. And Crockett was missing.

"The sly dog."

"Who?" Nina asked Navarro.

"Never mind. I'll be right back."

Navarro left the kitchen and headed upstairs. Crockett was in the second-floor rumpus room, his boots kicked off, his face under a *Playboy* magazine. The very picture of relaxation.

Navarro knocked the magazine off his brother's face and then rescued it before it hit the floor. "No napping during family trauma time."

"I'm keeping myself serene," Crockett said, his tone injured. "I'm waiting for you to come up with a new angle to The Plan, now that we've brought Nina and Valentine here. I suspect you're now wanting Valentine and Last to talk this out like mature adults?"

Navarro leaned against a wall, idly thumbing through the *Playboy.* "Too much to hope for, probably. I think we should focus on the final goal, what we want to achieve."

"What about Nina?"

Navarro sighed. "Why does it feel like I've known her for six years?" He pawed his hair. "She's intense for a merely peachy kind of girl."

"I think you shot through peachy with her a few hours ago. Now you're more into the pit of the relationship. The hard part. People get touchy when long-term goals are being discussed. And I don't have to tell you," Crockett said, "when a baby is thrown into the mix, matters usually get fairly elaborate."

Navarro shook his head. "This was supposed to be a tag-team thing. It's your turn."

"My turn to what?"

"Keep an eye on Nina."

"You're doing fine," Crockett said. "Besides, it's Valentine we were keeping an eye on. Her sister was just the conduit of accidental good fortune. The ladder, if you will, to get inside the burning house."

"Yes, yes, well, now I need to take some heat off. Go watch Nina and make sure the whole ranch doesn't catch on fire if Last and Valentine decide to get over-unfond of each other."

"I don't want a turn. I want to reward my reconnaissance trip with a nap."

"You can't go through life eating cupcakes and snoozing under *Playboy*. I need to think. Relinquish the sofa and go moderate downstairs."

Crockett sat up. "Wait a minute. You're not going sweet on Nina, are you? Like, really sweet?"

"Hell, no."

"Hell, yes, you are," Crockett said.

"I swear I am not. I may be mildly attracted to her—mildly—but I am *not* going sweet." Navarro gave his brother his most annoyed glance. "Nor is she one bit sweet on me."

"Well, *that* I believe."

Irritation flooded through Navarro. "So, can I have a break from our project? One of us should be down there to keep an eye on Last."

"Actually, I've been thinking that he's got to learn to face his own issues, Navarro. We've been facing them for him for years."

"Whatever." Navarro slapped his palm with the rolled-up *Playboy*. "I never knew having women around could be so disturbing."

Crockett got up and took the *Playboy*. "Easy on Miss May, bro. Sure, I'll take over for you. No problem. It'll be a pleasure to watch Nina."

Navarro snatched the magazine back and took his brother's place on the sofa. Kicking off his boots, he lay down, sighing deeply as he opened the centerfold over his face.

Crockett sighed. "It's only paper, bro."

"Paper has its pluses, too," Navarro murmured. "Paper dolls don't argue with you. Don't let Nina make you crazy."

"I won't. Enjoy your snooze."

He would—except for worrying about his twin and his twin's love of all things sweet.

NINA WATCHED one of the twin brothers come back into the kitchen. He had changed his shirt. All the cowboys wore the same basic attire, as if they all used the same laundry basket and grabbed whatever was clean that day. He'd changed and freshened up, and the grin he threw her was positively conspiracy-sharing.

It was Crockett. "Where's your brother? Everybody's waiting so that we can talk about what we're going to do about…you know."

"Nah," he said. "We're not going to talk about that today. We avoid deep discussions the first day we meet someone."

"Oh." Nina was surprised. "Okay. I thought they were waiting on your brother before they got serious."

Because there was nothing serious about

any of the brothers. The awkward silence had disappeared and now they were all eating cupcakes and laughing—except Last, who looked slightly ill. Neither he nor Valentine glanced toward each other. Nina felt sorry for both of them. "I think things might move along if your brother joined the family caucus," she said.

"No, he'd only slow things down. Cupcake?"

She shook her head.

"You're missing out. Mmm." Crockett ate his cupcake with an expression of sheer joy on his face.

These men were all boys. Now that she'd made it to the ranch and seen how they lived, her duty was clear. No way were these emotionally stunted men of Malfunction Junction going to raise her sister's child. She frowned, thinking about the man of mystery who'd napped under his hat and then brought her sister to the ranch. He was the wild card. He might be an adult. There might be hope here, gold yet uncovered. She owed it to him to find out before she made her decision regarding her niece's or nephew's future.

No one was looking at her. They were all busy eating cupcakes. Calhoun was pouring milk for Valentine.

Nina left the kitchen and crept up the stairs.

"Hello," she said. "Anybody here?" Her blood pounding in her ears, she walked to the end of the hall.

And there he was, Mr. Mystery, stretched out on a sofa with a *Playboy* magazine on his face.

What a rascal.

She had to admit she found his elusiveness exciting, and, for a librarian, the fact that he hid behind printed reading matter was a bonus. Her pulse raced as she approached him. Miss May smiled up at her in a provocative pose. A light snore came from under the pages.

How many men would she ever meet who were comfortable snoozing with a centerfold on his face?

He can use my lacy lavender thong as a bookmark anytime.

"Hello," Nina whispered. "Yoo-hoo."

Navarro's eyes widened as he recognized Nina's voice above the magazine. "What do you want?"

"To see you when I talk to you."

No way. He'd feel vulnerable without his disguise.

"Do you know you have a nudie magazine on your face?"

What did she expect in a houseful of men? *Ladies' Home Journal?*

Come to think of it, Last had been known to swipe a copy of that from their next door neighbor, Mimi. He said he liked looking at the recipes, but Navarro had always suspected it was the feeling of hominess the magazine projected that warmed Last's heart. "Do I really? What a strange thing. I thought I'd picked up the copy of *Southern Living* I was reading only yesterday."

"Shall I remove it for you?" Nina asked.

"No, thank you. Black ink is black ink. The words aren't important, but they make a great nightshade." He figured that would be an insult to a card-carrying, card-cataloging librarian.

"That's all right," she said. "I feel like I'm talking to the phantom in the *Phan-*

tom of the Opera. I actually like not seeing your face, Crockett."

Oh, boy. There went her romantic escapism problem again. *And* she'd confused
him with his twin.

"Everybody's downstairs, except you.
Do you always ignore your family?"

His eyes widened. If she only knew
how much he did not ignore his family.
"Mmm." He grunted.

"I don't know about you guys," Nina
said.

Navarro rolled his eyes under the magazine.

Then her voice, tinged with that slight
edge of smart-aleck that he felt so chal-
lenged, bedeviled and intrigued by, continued. "Navarro insists you all are going to
raise Valentine's baby, but frankly, I don't
see a baby fitting into your lifestyle." She
sighed. "Navarro doesn't know what he's
talking about."

Ha! Navarro knew exactly what he was
talking about!

"In fact," Nina said, "I don't think he
knows *what* he wants. *You,* on the other
hand, Crockett, *you* know you want to

relax with a magazine on your face, and you just do it. I *admire* that."

Was she hitting on him? On *Crockett?* She was, the little minx! He could feel the pages start to steam around his face as his breathing picked up. She was sweet-talking his twin!

Now he understood his little peach. She wasn't all Dewey decimal systems and matronly attributes. She had a severe case of wanting a bad boy.

Of course, he was an original, from a long line of boys who knew the real meaning of bad.

Navarro reached out, grabbed Nina and pulled her onto him. He kept the magazine plastered over their heads, but he pulled Nina's face close enough to his for a lip-locking, breath-stealing, bad-boy kiss.

She didn't even fight him for the paper canopy. Instead her hands held his face and, since she was on top—surely her favorite position, bossy girl that she was— she took over the kiss. Her lips touched his, stole his breath, and heated his blood. His hand stole down to her fanny. Damn, it was a peach, just as he'd suspected.

He was about to throw Miss May to the wall and really get moving with the bad boy romantic escapism Nina was craving when he heard a throat clear in the doorway.

Nina jumped away.

He kept the magazine over his face, praying they hadn't been caught by one of his brothers. They'd never let him hear the end of it!

"Sorry," Valentine said. "I was looking for the powder room. Nina, I think you're needed downstairs."

He pointed back to the hallway, gesturing that Valentine should have turned left to find the powder room.

The room was silent, and after he heard Valentine close the powder room door, he peeked out from underneath Miss May.

Nina was gone.

"And once again, I am left thinking about her," he muttered. "Darn that crazy little package of misfortune!"

A man could not keep a close enough eye on her.

He almost felt a need to stay right next

to her at all times, to make certain he could keep his eyes and hands on her.

Just to keep her out of trouble, of course.

"What's so important down there?" he muttered. If Valentine had come to get Nina, then he needed to be down there, too. Though he'd wanted to tag-team, Navarro knew that Crockett couldn't be trusted with the details, nor to make decisions. In fact, no one could be trusted to make decisions where Nina was concerned—she and her sister were quite the duo of explosive drama, and only he knew it!

"Darn," he said, pulling on his boots. "It isn't easy being a man of mystery *and* a man of responsibility." He dialed Crockett's cell phone so he could tell him to come back up to swap places with him. "Best if those two spend as little time around each other as possible—specifically since Nina's obviously got a twin bad boy fantasy thing disturbing her."

"Hello," Crockett said.

"I've decided you need to nap. I'll handle the family caucus."

"I'm good," Crockett said. "You enjoy Miss May."

"Get back up here before I have a coronary!"

"Not right now," Crockett said. "I'm just getting to the good stuff."

"What good stuff?"

"You know."

"No, I don't know," Navarro said, sensing where the conversation was going. "Tell me you're not cozying up to Nina."

"Vice versa, in fact."

He sounded way too happy about that. "Get up here," Navarro demanded. "You don't understand what you're getting yourself into."

"Can't be all that bad," Crockett said. "No woman is."

Navarro ground his teeth. "No tag-team dating our girlfriend," Navarro reminded him. "No dating her at all!"

"I dunno. She's a free woman, isn't she? You're not interested in getting tied down. And you told me to keep an eye on her." He paused for a second. "My eyes like what they see, actually."

Navarro squinted. "Crockett, when next I see you, I'm going to put my boot up your jeans."

"You may never see me again," Crockett said. "Nina's just about convinced me to move to Delaware."

"That's it," Navarro said. "I'm coming down."

Crockett laughed. "Cool off, hothead. It would be an inefficient use of time. I'm handling what you assigned me."

"That was back when I thought efficiency was the better part of planning," Navarro said. "Now I think I better not delegate Nina."

"I think your goat's being got, bro. I think you may like that little girl more than you're letting on."

"Is she standing right there listening to you? Because I'm pretty sure you're wrong, and I wouldn't want her disappointed. She only *thinks* she's falling for my Man of Mystery routine."

Crockett laughed so hard he had a coughing attack. "Gotta go," he said between wheezes. "See ya."

Navarro clicked off, annoyed. He spread the magazine back over his face, but for some reason, he'd lost the urge to nap.

Nina's giggle floated up the stairs.

Crockett was probably doing his thing, making her laugh at his antics. That was the problem with his twin; he had all the seriousness of a clown. Navarro hardly ever cracked a joke, and he couldn't remember a punch line to save his soul.

Another giggle. "That's it," Navarro said. "Back doors were made for situations like this. I'm going riding, and I'm not coming back until everybody is in bed!"

TWO HOURS LATER, Nina knew matters were far from being resolved. Valentine was uncomfortable, and Last was miserable. The two of them didn't belong in the same room together. The doctor had long since left, after kindly chatting with Valentine and reassuring her. No one wanted to talk about what they were going to do about the baby, and the Man of Mystery was remaining elusive—despite her pretending to kiss his brother.

Jealousy was not in Navarro's dictionary. He might be a great kisser, but if she fell for his appeal, her position would be as unfortunate as her sister's.

Reality had to kick in sometime.

"Let's go to bed, Valentine," Nina said softly, patting her sister's hand.

"Great idea."

Nina nodded. "Gentlemen, my sister and I are going to call it a night." She stood, forcing a smile for everyone. Of all the brothers, she had to say she was most disappointed in Navarro. Gone was the camaraderie they'd shared earlier in the day. Though she didn't deny the situation was awkward, she missed the easygoing banter they'd explored.

It was almost as if he'd turned into a different person once he'd returned to Malfunction Junction. And now he'd been gone for nearly two hours.

She was finding it very easy to be peeved with him.

She noticed Last hanging back in the family room so he wouldn't have to say good-night to them.

"Here," Crockett said. "I'll walk you to the other house."

"We'll be fine," Nina said. "We actually don't mind walking alone. It'll give us time to wind down."

He handed her the keys and a flashlight. "Can I at least follow you?"

She shook her head. "We'll be fine. Watch from the window."

The brothers watched them from the porch. "You did fine," she said to Valentine, squeezing her hand as they walked.

"I barely said a word. I was too nervous." Valentine looked at her. "I shouldn't have come. It didn't solve anything."

"It's too soon to solve anything. Everything's difficult." They walked onto the main road.

Valentine started to cry. "I wish I weren't in this position."

"I wish we weren't, either, but we are, and it's all going to be fine. I, for one, cannot wait to hold the baby."

"I think that cowboy would be falling for you if I wasn't in the way," Valentine said. "I've messed up your chance to have a man love you."

"Nonsense," Nina said, walking faster. "Navarro's not The One, anyway. I have a funny feeling that happiness is *not* dating a Jefferson male. Although he does kiss *very* well."

"THE JIG IS UP," Crockett told his twin as he walked into the barn later that night. "I found you. May I rate you an F for Hospitality to Guests In Difficult Times?"

Navarro grunted. "Put a sock in it, Crockett. Everything happened too fast. Decisions were flying and actions that required consideration were stampeding. I needed a time-out."

"You knew they were tricky girls," Crockett pointed out.

"I didn't realize they could play the game at white-hot speed. Why didn't I believe myself when I said that carefully thinking through our actions was important?"

"And yet, what would going slower have gotten you? I don't know, man," Crockett said, biting into another cupcake. "I still say we came out with more info about Valentine's plans than we had going in."

Navarro looked at his brother. "You have frosting on your chin."

Crockett wiped off the frosting. "I like Valentine," he said with a shrug. "She's a bit tough, but she's had to be. Mostly she just thinks about her baby."

Navarro groaned. "This isn't going to be easy, is it?"

"Nope."

"I can't even see the finish line now."

"We didn't see it when we started. It's just farther away than we'd hoped it would be by now."

"What are we going to do about Last?"

"Not a damn thing," Crockett said. "We let him solve his own problems. He got himself into this. Perhaps we shouldn't go rushing in to save the day." He shrugged. "The day can't be saved, anyway. We're having a baby."

"Darn that charmed bed," Navarro said. *And darn Nina for making me want to sleep in it with her!*

"Stay out of it," Crockett told him. "I don't believe in charms, good luck or otherwise, but we don't need to test fate."

"I don't think I'll be invited into Nina's bed even if I figure out how to rescue it." He'd be lucky if he ever got Nina out on a date. "I should get some sleep. I have a lot to do tomorrow."

"What's our plan now?"

Navarro shook his head. "To put this

horse up." He patted the animal's neck. "After that, there's no telling."

"What about Nina?"

"She went off mad. What can a man do with an angry female?"

Crockett laughed. "Not a damn thing except stay out of the way."

"Thanks for the help. You're a regular ray of sunshine."

"Yep." Crockett took the horse's reins and began walking toward the stall. "Strange thing, being related by a baby."

"It happens all the time."

"Yes, but with Valentine there'll be no wedding. No Christmas dinners. And it feels so wrong to have relatives who don't like us. I say our new plan should be to woo Valentine."

"You're joking, right?"

"Not exactly," Crockett said carefully. "Last can't handle this deal. You saw him. He looked like he had spiders in his pants the whole time Valentine was here. In fact, he's been weirded out ever since he learned he's going to be a father."

"He probably knows Mason's gonna bust a cap when he comes home and finds out

Last didn't recite the condom poem Mason drummed into our heads way back when we still thought rubbers were something to be used for schoolwork and rolling up newspapers."

"Sure. Mason will freak, no question. Best we get the problem cleaned up before our oldest brother returns," Crockett said. "As much as it can be cleaned up, anyway. That means the baby belongs here, too."

"I hear what you're saying." Nina had made it clear she was headed back to Delaware. "I did hear Valentine tell Nina that she needed to buzz off about the baby plans. Valentine's getting all maternal and protective now that something's growing inside her."

"Sure she is. Valentine's not a lost cause," Crockett said. "We need to convince her that Union Junction is the place for her and her baby. Not some salon of questionable repute. Or Delaware."

"What about her request for funds? Don't suppose it'll ever pop back up again?"

"Maybe she'd rather have a family and a clean, safe home for her baby than sue us,"

Crockett pointed out. "Maybe she'd rather have a father figure."

"Whoa." Navarro watched his brother remove the saddle from the horse. "Father figure?"

"Most women count two parents as an essential hope for their child. We are the only family who thinks we're just fine without the maternal component. But then again, we've always had Mimi, and she gave us the female counterpoint we needed."

"Mimi," Navarro muttered. "Now there's an example of love gone wrong. Mason pushed her into another man's arms."

"What the hell?" Crockett said. "Earth to Navarro, fast, please."

"Crap. I'm at risk of becoming Mason," Navarro said. "Is it possible to become Mason, when you've tried so hard not to?"

"I don't know, bro. Have you been overlooking your best friend for umpteen years? Did the little girl in pigtails who stole your hunting guns turn into the county's best-looking woman when you had your head up a cow's behind?" Crockett stared at him.

Navarro took a deep breath. "I've only known her for a day, but I'm still afraid I screwed everything up."

"Well, you did," Crockett agreed cheerfully. "Royally. And may I point out that you did it in a record twelve hours. That may be a Jefferson cake-taker. But, look at it this way. It was *only* twelve hours. It's impossible to lose your sanity over a woman in that short amount of time."

"Not if you factor in the love-at-first-sight expediator."

"Expediator?" Crockett guffawed. "Is that *Webster's* or *Oxford*?"

"No dictionary at all. I'm serious! I believe in love at first sight. I mean," Navarro hedged, "I'm not saying I'm *in love* or anything." He took a deep breath. "But I'm willing to admit there's a possibility I don't know everything."

"You know enough to make up words," Crockett said with a grin. "You always sucked at Scrabble."

"I am saying I'd like that little peach in my fruit basket." Navarro forked some hay into the bin. "I don't want to romance Valentine. The importance of Valentine cannot be understated, since she's bearing Jefferson offspring. But I have an itch for Nina I swear I can't scratch."

Crockett sighed. "She'll go back to Delaware and break your heart. It's a very bad idea, Navarro. I'd buy myself a backscratcher if I was you and do the job yourself."

Navarro gave him a black look. "You romance Valentine. Nina's already confused enough about who she was kissing for me to go romancing her sister. All I need is for Nina to think I play from both sides of the street."

"Um, no." Crockett shook his head. "She wouldn't think that."

"I don't want to talk about it any more. She's funny. She's cute. She's round and soft. She's sexy. She's smart—librarians like her just don't grow on trees around here," Navarro said. He sat on a bench.

Last walked into the barn, his dog at his side. "Where have you guys been?"

"Hanging around," Navarro said. "How are you holding up?"

"I think I'm better now," Last said. "I

only saw Valentine that one night and I was afraid to face her again."

Navarro looked at him. "You never knew her at all? Even I've seen Valentine hanging around the rodeos."

"Be honest. We've all seen her at the front desk of the Never Lonely Cut-n-Gurls salon," Crockett said. "Let's quit lying to each other. We've all been in there for a trim. We may love Delilah across the street, and our loyalty may be to her salon, but we've all been inside the competition for a look-see. Some of us have even gotten more than that."

"I never went in," Last said. "When I go To Lonely Hearts Station, I visit and drink tea with Delilah and Jerry."

"Then how did it happen?" Crockett asked. "You can skip the most sordid of the details."

"He can't skip too many," Navarro said. "Because I had to put the bed back together. I know he's not as innocent as he looks."

"There was no bed." Last shook his head. "I was at Barmaid's Creek. Somehow I ended up there after the rodeo party Marvella threw at her place."

Crockett and Navarro stared at each other.

"Are you certain?" Navarro asked.

"I'm pretty sure the only time I was conscious that night after I was drinking was when I was in the creek," Last said. "I was pickled."

"His jeans *were* wet when he got home," Crockett said. "I thought he'd been swimming in the heart-shaped hot tub, which, as yet, I have not experienced."

"I think the taxi came for me at the creek," Last said. "I'm sure there's records at the taxi office. The town is not that big."

Navarro's face went stonelike. "I've been had," he said.

"What do you mean?" Crockett demanded.

"That little story-time-tellin' librarian with a penchant for avoiding twenty questions knows more than she's telling."

AT A SOUND BEHIND THEM, Valentine turned. "What's that coming up the road?" she asked. "It looks like a man on a horse."

"I was just thinking the same thing." Nina slowed her pace to peer at it. "It *is* a man on a horse, riding fast. Can you believe how fast he's going? I would never ride that fast on a horse. In fact, I don't even like horses. Contrary beasts."

She moved as tight to the shoulder of the road as she could and stopped so she wouldn't spook the horse. To her surprise, the horse pulled up and Navarro grinned down at her.

The Navarro she remembered from this morning, with sparkling eyes and gnarly attitude.

"Forget something?" Nina asked.

"Nope."

"What's the matter, Lassie? Tree in the road? Timmie take a spill? Speak, Lassie," she said, annoyed that Navarro looked so good and so manly astride his black horse.

He actually chuckled at her. "Think you left too soon."

"Really? You mean, the party's about to get better?"

"Maybe."

She shook her head. "We're tired, Navarro. This has all been very stressful on my sister. We want to go to bed."

"Give us a chance," he said. "We don't do well around women. But we can find some manners, even me. And I'll probably improve as I get the hang of it." He tipped his hat to Valentine. "Miss Valentine."

Nina blinked. "Valentine wants a comfy bed and a hot shower."

"I do?" Valentine asked.

"Yes. Not too hot, of course, just right."

"Then let me visit you later. After you've had some time to unwind."

"Why?"

His shrug was confident. "To talk about baby booties and cribs and stuff."

"Suppose Valentine doesn't want to talk about that?"

"Then we just get to know each other better over a game of Ping-Pong. A back-and-forth game between two combatants." He laughed after he said it, and Nina narrowed her eyes.

"You're too slippery," she said. "I have a funny feeling you're not giving the full story on a lot of stuff."

He winked. "I'm harmless."

"No, you're not."

"You like him," Valentine said in a low voice. "He's sexy."

Nina peered up at Navarro. "Sexy doesn't do me any good if there isn't honesty to go with it," she said to Valentine.

"I heard that," Navarro said. "Honesty is the best policy."

"He likes you, too," Valentine said. "Men don't grin like that unless they're interested."

"Or unless they're working an angle." Nina shook her head. "Hit the road, cowboy. We've got to go, and you're messing up the benefits of our exercise."

"I've been working on a list of suggestions."

Nina raised a brow. "Suggestions? Did we ask for any? This should be new and different," she said to Valentine.

"Roll with it," her sister said. "I like the way he looks at you."

"Repeat after me. Nina is not looking for a one-night stand…Nina is not looking for a one-night stand."

"What if he's more than that?" Valentine asked. "What if he's the hearth-and-home kind?"

Nina shook her head. "No. He's not."

"There are a few thoughts on my mind," Navarro said, ignoring their fast and furious whispering. "Pardon me for saying so, Miss Valentine, but I think the first thing that needs to happen is that you find a job here in Union Junction. The Union Junction Stylists are one option, as well as Lampy's, if you know your way around a bar. The owner has a good heart."

Nina handed Valentine the door keys to house number three. "You go on," she told her. "I'm going to slap this cowboy."

"But—"

"No buts. He's so pigheaded and bossy that he thinks he can make decisions for you."

"So do you!"

Nina looked at her sister. "What do you mean? Oh." Nina let out a deep sigh of tired tension. "We did talk about this earlier. Sorry."

Navarro cleared his throat to get their attention. "Hello?"

"You go on back to the ranch, cowboy," Nina said. "Thank you for your input."

"Things have to be discussed, Nina."

"Obviously. But not in the order in which any of us thought they would be discussed, probably." She patted Valentine's hand.

"Ride back with me, Nina," Navarro said. "We need to talk."

She looked at him, surprised. "I need to be with my sister."

"And I really need to be alone," Valentine said. "Truly, Nina, I don't want to have a heart-to-heart now. Coming out here was the best thing I could have done. It's cleared my mind about a lot of things. Now I want to think about what's best for me and my child."

Nina hesitated. "What are you saying?"

"You go with Navarro. That horse will hold two."

"No," Nina said, "sisters stay together." In a low aside to Valentine, she said, "I know what you're doing. Quit playing matchmaker!"

"I'm not! But there's no reason for you to baby-sit me."

Navarro backed the horse up a few steps,

then brought it alongside the women again. "Valentine, you're part of our family now."

Valentine looked worried.

"There are plenty of nice places in town. We could help you find a duplex or something where you and the baby could live."

Nina stared at him. "I don't know if I'm angry or grateful that you're trying to be nice."

"I'm not really trying to be nice. I'm trying to find a solution that works for everybody, and most especially, the baby."

"It's for me and my sister to decide what will be best for her and the baby. Goodbye, Navarro," Nina said. She took the keys from Valentine, walked up the driveway and opened the front door. "He has lost his mind."

Valentine shook her head. "Don't you like him just a little?"

Nina looked behind her, seeing the cowboy on his horse in the center of the road, watching them leave him alone. She sighed. "Navarro and my heart are going to have to decide that I only feel sisterly toward him. I can't survive this much passion."

"Sisterly?"

"The kiss you interrupted earlier was good. Think Elizabeth Taylor and Richard Burton rolling around in the sand."

"Yikes! Did you like it?"

"Curiously, yes. I liked the whole bad cowboy fantasy. Now I've got it out of my system." She glanced at Valentine. "All I can tell you is that everything I thought was true when I came here a few hours ago has now changed. It's time to regroup."

Valentine glanced over her shoulder. "Regroup quickly."

"Why?"

"Because Dark Rider's coming after you and the only thing he's missing is a cape."

"Oh, for pity's sake!" Nina stopped. "Now what?" she said to him, appreciating the view of sweaty male and strong thighs gripping the saddle as he aligned the horse beside the porch. "We're never going to get any sleep at this rate."

"You wanted to kiss my twin brother," Navarro said. "So, I want you to know that, even though he has his good sides, he's my evil twin. We went to Lonely Hearts Station to keep an eye on Valentine. Between the two of us, we figured it would be an easy job." He stared down at Nina. "The truth is, it wasn't. Now, you and I are on the same team, and I never want you to think we aren't. Of course, that doesn't include kissing Crockett."

Nina blinked, her breath stolen by his emotional comment.

"I was the man under the *Playboy.* You kissed me, and I'd like clarity on what you think about my brother. Because you're only going to kiss *me* from now on."

Chapter Six

"Go talk to him, Nina," Valentine said. "I could use a few minutes to myself, anyway."

"I'll take good care of her," Navarro said. "Come on, Nina. Let's see how you ride."

"Not very well," she muttered, which made him laugh. "Not at all, in fact."

"Okay." He didn't care how poorly she rode, just so long as she gave him some time. "Not back there, up front, where I can keep an eye on you," he said, helping her into the saddle.

The instant she slid between his thighs, he felt better. "Agreeable little thing you are."

"Hush. This makes me very nervous."

She clutched at the reins. Putting his hands over hers, he said, "Relax."

"With you? Not likely."

Valentine laughed. "See you later, Nina. Good night, Navarro."

He wheeled the horse around and headed toward the road. She was stiff and anxious, so he slid an arm around her waist. "See? Good horsie. Nothing to be afraid of."

"How does it see in the dark?"

"Ah, Librarian Lady. Have you spent all your life in your ivory tower of books and dreams?"

"Yes," Nina said curtly, "and I liked it there very well."

"Safe and snug."

She tried not to lean back against his chest. "If you wish to define it that way."

"Did you know that a horse can tell whether a woman is honest?"

"Ugh. No teasing and word games right now, Navarro. I have to focus on praying that the horse doesn't decide to run."

He laughed, then clicked to the horse. As the horse began to canter and then to gallop, he held Nina tighter to him.

"Stop, Navarro! Stop! Oh, my God, stop!" she shrieked.

Chuckling, he slowed the horse to a canter and then a walk again.

"Let me down," she said through teeth that sounded clenched. "You're despicable."

"Just making sure you get that blood flowing. Next time you read a romance novel where the hero snatched the woman away on his charger, you'll remember me." He smiled as he blocked her from trying to slide from the horse. "Be a good sport, Nina. Fire Demon tells me you're honest and therefore you pass his test and may ride him."

"Is that really his name? Fire Demon?"

He laughed. "Nah. I just thought it would pique your story-loving heart. His name is George. Curious George."

"Does it seem wrong to name your horse after a monkey?"

"Ah," Navarro said, happy that she hadn't noticed he was still holding her against him tightly. He could feel the stiffness in her body relaying her fear. Taking advantage of a librarian's fear of runaway horses might be dirty pool, but the rewards were definitely in the pocket. "I am more well read than you think, as I've illustrated. My dad read us those books. I loved the man in the yellow hat. Hats make the man, and his was large and yellow."

"Was there a visual connection for you?"

"Yes. I always wanted my hat to be big. And I wanted to have a monkey to pal around with. Other than Crockett, of course."

She giggled and he felt a little of the tension leave her body.

"Wanna make out?" he asked.

"No!"

He laughed and dropped kisses along the curve of her shoulder. "Methinks you doth protest too much. Name the author."

"I—"

"Shh," Navarro said. A strange sound came to him. "Do you hear that?"

"No," she said sternly.

"Okay. It was probably the wind." He focused on Nina again, happy that he had her right where he wanted her—practically in his lap. "Nina, there's something I have to ask you, and there's no easy way to do this, but Last says that he doesn't remember being alone with your sister."

"So he's claiming he's not the father?" Nina's tone was outraged.

"Hang on, peach," Navarro said. "A paternity test after the baby is born will answer that question, and then I'll beat Last myself if he's lying." Navarro hesitated. "Did you hear that? I *know* I heard something."

"It sounded like a bush coughing," Nina whispered. "But I don't think that's possible."

"Bushes only cough in fantasy novels. I'd better go see what needs to clear its throat. Care to investigate with me?"

"Sure. I'm already in this adventure up to my eyeballs."

"You have no idea." He pulled the horse alongside a row of possibly guilty bushes, giving each of them a strong kick with his boot.

"Do you think that's a good idea?" Nina asked. "What if something reaches out and grabs you?"

"I'll expect you to rescue me." He slid off the horse and peered into the bushes.

"What are you *doing*?"

"Just taking a breather. In fact, I need

to take a leak. I think I'll just unzip my jeans and take a leak into these coughing bushes—"

"No!" Last called from the ground. He tried to rise and fell over. "Oh, God," he moaned. "I'm seeing stars. And maybe angel's wings."

"You're not seeing stars," Navarro said, reaching through the scratchy bushes to haul his brother to his feet. "Possibly litter. And more likely cobwebs than angel wings. What the hell are you doing?"

Last squinted, trying to focus on Nina. "Where's your shishter?"

"Last," Navarro said, "this has got to stop."

"Nothing's got to stop," Last replied. "Nothing at all." He leaned to the right, tried to pull himself up and fell forward suddenly, spooking the horse. Nina yelped when the horse jumped and she clutched at the horse's mane wildly, which made it take off at a dead run. She hung on for dear life, trapped in a nightmare she couldn't stop. "Whoa!" she yelled. "Whoa, damn it!"

Maybe a mile later, gasping, realizing

she had no idea how to stop the horse, she squeezed her eyes shut and pulled back on the horse's head with all her strength.

The horse responded by stopping so fast she vaulted over its head. "Aieee!" she cried, landing on the ground to peer up at the sky overhead. Tears streamed from the sides of her eyes as she took stock of her body. "Ankles move, legs move, arms move, head is a bit dizzy but still attached to neck. Blasted beast," she told the horse, which couldn't have cared less about her as it wandered away.

"Carcass of doom," she told it as she struggled to sit up. "And curses on the cowboy who talked me into getting up on your sloping back."

Nina looked around her, fairly convinced that she was in better shape than she'd expected. "And luck is with me," she said. "Here is my house, and I am going inside," she told her nemesis. "Possibly I should call your owner, but this is your ranch, and I think you'll be fine. I could whack you on the rear and tell you to go home, but I don't like having my rear slapped, so I'll assume you don't, either. Good night," she finished, her pride more wounded than anything as she ungraciously got to her feet and headed inside to her sister.

"I just had some sense knocked into me," Nina said to Valentine when she entered the house. Her sister had on a nice comfy robe, she'd showered and her hair was up in a floppy bun. She was the picture of happiness.

"We have choices," Nina continued. "I'm not sure ranch life suits me." Nina picked leaves from her hair. It was nice of the boys to vacate one of their ranch houses for them, but still, it wasn't home. "We do not have to stay here."

"I know." Valentine nodded and went to put a teakettle on the stove. "And I know you're not keen on staying. I'll consider whatever suggestion you make." She glanced at her sister. "I'm sorry you're having to worry about me so much."

Nina shook her head. "It doesn't matter. Everything's going to work out." She seated herself on a plaid sofa, under a pair of deer antlers. "What does one call those?" she asked Valentine. "A pair? A bunch? Just antlers?"

"I don't know," Valentine said, shaking her head. "I try not to look at them. Ranch life is something I'm going to have to learn."

"Does that mean you would consider staying here permanently?" Nina asked.

Her sister came to sit beside her, setting each of them a teacup on the coffee table. "I'm still trying to figure out the pregnancy cycle. Having a baby scares me. Tonight I'm enjoying not living with Marvella. She got scary there at the end." Taking a deep breath, she said, "Nina, I'm sorry we had to leave the bed behind. I should never have brought it here. It should have stayed with you. You're so much more stable than I am. But, crazily, now that I'm here I feel like I've found a home."

"I'm going to bed," Nina said crossly. "And if the cowboy comes looking for me, tell him I wouldn't have his stupid horse if he paid me. Good might."

Valentine laughed. "Good night."

IN THE MORNING, a knock at the door startled the sisters as they fixed breakfast in the sunny kitchen.

"Visitors," Nina said, patting her sister's hand as she left the room. "I think the menfolk would call before they showed up, so I guess we should answer it and let whoever it is know that the menfolk are at the other house."

"You sound just like Mrs. Cartwright," Valentine called after her. "Menfolk."

"I'm trying to fit in here." Nina opened the door. "Hello," she said to the attractive blonde on the porch, trying not to have a huge leap of jealousy since this was Navarro's house and clearly the blonde knew where he lived. "The menfolk are up at the main house." She eyed the small baby in the blonde's arms. "Pretty baby."

"Thank you." The blonde smiled at her and Nina tried not to like her. "The *menfolk* sent me here to see you and your sister. By the way, nobody really refers to the Jefferson brothers as 'menfolk.' We'd more likely call them mentalfolk." She laughed. "My name is Mimi. I'm the next-door neighbor. And this," she said, holding up the baby, "is Nanette."

"I'm Nina Cakes, and this is my sister, Valentine. Come on in."

"Hi, Mimi," Valentine said, rising. "Can I get you a cup of tea?"

"I'd love one." Mimi sat in the chair opposite the sofa, cradling her sleeping baby.

Nina couldn't help smiling at the motherly love on Mimi's face. "Is she your only child?"

"Yes. Thank you," she said as Valentine put a teacup on the table in front of her. "I hear you're expecting one of these angels."

Valentine nodded. "How did you hear?"

"Navarro called. He told me I might want to come over and meet you." Mimi smiled. "Just in case you wanted to talk 'baby stuff' or 'woman stuff' or any other 'stuff' ladies liked to talk about. 'Stuff' was the main word he seemed comfortable using."

"That was kind of sweet of him," Valentine said. "Don't you think that was thoughtful, Nina?"

"Yes," she said reluctantly, "very much so, actually." It was surprising that Navarro would think to send a woman over to greet them and to offer Valentine the opportunity to talk "baby stuff" with a new mother. "Thank you for coming over,

Mimi. We may not stay at the ranch long, but it's nice to have another woman to talk to."

"He also mentioned that you had a horse disaster last night. He said he was sorry he couldn't come make sure you were all right, but he had to get Last home." She smiled. "Actually he said you were a common-sense girl and would call the ranch if you needed him. Were you hurt?"

"Not by the horse," Nina said. "Mostly, it was just injured pride."

Mimi raised a brow. "Navarro seems to think you're staying for a long time. He talked about getting Valentine in with my doctor for prenatal care. You'd like her," Mimi continued. "She's very smart, Valentine, and young, but sharp—"

"Hold on," Nina said. "Did he really say that?"

"Yes." Mimi nodded. "Are you upset?"

"I believe so," Nina said. "He's managing my sister's life."

"No, he's not," Valentine said. "Just a minute ago you said he was being thoughtful."

"Yes, but it is thoughtful to send a friend

over. It is managing to arrange for prenatal care." Nina sighed. "He's possessed by the baby, I swear."

Mimi laughed. "It's a family trait."

"Really?" Nina sat up. "It's going to get old fast."

"I'd like to make my own decisions," Valentine said. "I would love to begin prenatal care with your doctor, Mimi. Thank you."

"Oh, rats," Nina said. "Why is it I'm supposed to butt out but Navarro the Nice is not?"

"Because he's making sense and you're not," Valentine said. "My sister's having a bit of a block toward that man."

"Really?" Mimi perked up. "Something I should know about?"

"I think you already know that Jefferson men, apparently, revel in their reputation for alarming pigheadedness, raw determination and scare tactics. Need I say more?"

"And that bothers you?" Mimi asked. "So you've decided to take charge of your family?"

"Exactly." Nina nodded. "Thank you for not painting me as the villainess."

"I completely understand," Mimi said with a smile. "But the truth is, you're probably fighting a losing battle."

"I cannot get comfortable with him," Nina said.

"You have a dilemma," Mimi said, taking a sip of her tea. Her gaze touched Nina's perplexed face. "Lavender peach. My all-time favorite. Very soothing." She touched Valentine's hand. "Please call me if you have any questions. My best advice right now is not to let stray pains upset you. They come and go, and it's usually gas," she said with a lowered voice and a wink. "Also, eat well. Lots of water—and lots of rest when you feel like it. Navarro says you've been through a lot, Valentine."

Okay, Nina thought, *I'm bowled over by his consideration. And I really, really don't want to be.*

"He has me right where he wants me," Nina said. "I'd look pretty stupid if I tried to drag Valentine away from consideration and care."

Mimi laughed. "They do have a way of winning the game. Not that this is a game, but…it's the Jefferson way to take care of their own."

"So Navarro told me, once upon a time," Nina said.

"A little advice for you, too?" Mimi said to Nina.

"Sure. Why not?"

Mimi stood, holding her baby close and putting her shawl back over the sleeping infant. "Jefferson love is something a lot of women would crawl miles on their belly to get. It's a special thing, when it happens, and believe me, it's as rare as finding gold in your backyard. So, if you're getting some Jefferson love, you should treasure it." She walked to the door, opening it to let herself out. "Because once you've thrown it away, all that gold is gone for good." She smiled at Valentine. "I'll be back again. Call me if you need anything."

"Thank you," Valentine said.

Mimi nodded at both women and then closed the door behind her.

"Whew," Valentine said. "She's a beauty."

"Yes," Nina said. "And let us not lose sight of the fact that she obviously didn't marry a Jefferson. Wonder why?"

"Maybe the neighbor thing got in the way," Valentine said. "But did you notice her tone changed when she talked about Jefferson 'love'? She sounded...sad."

Nina blinked. "Valentine, let's go back home," she said, hearing the desperation in her own voice.

Valentine leaned to place her head on Nina's shoulder. "I like it here. For the first time, I feel protected. It's been years since I've felt this way."

Me, too, Nina thought. *And it's really making me feel out of place.*

"THIS BED IS SUPPOSED to be charmed," Marvella said to her girls. "Charmed is good." Walking around it, she looked it over, her hands touching the carved wood and pretty linens. "It must be charmed, because it's going to bring me good luck."

One of her cats padded across the comforter. Marvella laughed. "Soft, isn't it? And yet springy when it counts." Sitting, she bounced lightly on the bed. "I see money in this bed."

She looked around the room where she'd stored Nina's prized possession. "I envision a new attraction at the next rodeo," Marvella said. "Anybody for Cowboy Bed Check?"

"'COWBOY BED CHECK,'" Crockett read two days later in the newspaper. "That sounds like a freaky new riding event."

"Not really," Navarro said. "I've been bed-checked many times." Right now he was being Nina-checked, after the horse-riding incident. He had apologized and generously decided to give her some space. Maybe after a few days of feeling at home, she'd settle down a bit.

She had a right to be peeved with him.

Crockett tossed him the newspaper, opened to where Navarro couldn't miss the picture of the bed with all Marvella's beautiful employees sitting in it, scantily clothed. "That's Nina's and Valentine's charmed bed! Their family heirloom!" Navarro read the ad. "'Which cowboy will stay in the ring the longest with the notorious BadAss Blue to win a date with the lady of your choice, in a romantic bed of your dreams?'"

Crockett grimaced. "That's not catch-the-calf, for sure."

"No, it's not a game for children," Navarro agreed. "This is not going to make Nina happy. She had plans for getting that bed back. Heck, *I* had plans for getting that bed back."

"And what would you do with it?" Crockett looked at him. "Think you need a charm?"

"No. Although, it couldn't hurt," Navarro said. "I just don't need one of the baby-making variety." He gazed at the ad thoughtfully for a moment. "You know, bedtime with Nina is an attractive thought."

Crockett laughed. "Bedtime with most women is an attractive thought."

"No, not most women," Navarro said. "I've been wondering if sex with one woman for the rest of my life is possible."

"Possible, or fun?"

"Do you think it would get old? I've always been worried about getting tired of the same thing over and over." He lowered his voice. "But then I think about waking up every morning with Nina, and I think maybe it would be a reason to worship."

"Dude." Crockett took the paper back. "Focus. Do you understand the position these women are in?"

"Seated? I don't mind seated. I can do seated."

Crockett shook his head. "The cowboys have to play chicken. Like they do when they sit at the table in the center of the arena and let the bull rush at them. The cowboy who stays the longest wins. Well, in this case, the cowboy who stays on the bed the longest wins."

"The bed's going to get smashed to pieces," Navarro said.

"Exactly."

"Don't tell Nina." Navarro scratched his face. "She's liable to do something crazy."

"A librarian? Do something crazy?"

Navarro put on his hat and stood. "You obviously haven't learned anything about librarians since meeting Nina."

"She likes order?"

"Yeah. And an heirloom, charmed, baby-for-sure bed is the crown amongst her possessions."

"Heavy is the head that wears the crown."

"Heavy is the heart that loses it." He gave his brother a haggard glance. "She'll never forgive me if Marvella succeeds at this revenge trick, since it's my brother at the heart of the problem."

"Not a way to start a relationship, I agree," Crockett said philosophically. "You could have done better."

"Thanks, bro," Navarro said. "Just remember, you're my twin. And I may ask you for a favor soon."

"Life is harsh."

"Tell me something I didn't know," Navarro said.

"CAN I TALK TO YOU?" Navarro said to Nina the next morning, when he located her in the kitchen of the main house. He was surprised she was here, but he wasn't going to waste time playing the strong, silent type.

It felt real good to have her in his house. He just wished what he had to tell her was good news.

She tasted the soup in the big pot that she'd filled with vegetables and spices.

"Hope you like potato soup. It's a family recipe."

"My stomach's growling. That's a yes."

"Good. I didn't know what to fix, and no one was here when I finally made it up to the main house this morning. I assume you keep normal ranch hours."

"Yeah. What time do librarians work?"

She shrugged. "It's mostly a day job. But I do a lot of research at night on my computer, too."

"Overtime."

She sent him a glance. "I prefer to think of it as being interested in my job. I love my job."

"When were you planning on going back?" Navarro asked.

"Very soon. I booked a one-way flight. No more trains and buses for me. And," she said, tapping Navarro with the spoon handle, "I'm going to call Marvella to ask her if she'll consider selling me the bed. After all, I think we're all clear on the fact that Marvella is all about money. So, I hired a small company to pick up the family bed from Lonely Hearts Station, pack it and ship it home. I'm looking forward to having it back where it belongs."

"Hang on a sec. I already offered her money. She didn't budge."

"Maybe because it was a Jefferson brother asking. And she was very mad at the time. It's a chance I have to take."

"I didn't think you'd leave Valentine."

Nina shrugged. "It's not an easy decision. I can come back after the baby is born to help her, though. To be honest, she wants to give living here a shot." She looked at Navarro. "And I realize I can't rescue her. She may be baby sister, but she needs to make her own choices." The lump in her throat was nearly unbearable.

"We'll take good care of her," Navarro said. "Nina, we *really* need to talk."

"We *are* talking, Navarro," Nina said. Maybe not about deep issues, but she was as deep as she could get right now.

He touched her and Nina felt a spark zap her. *Static electricity.* "It's a bad sign to experience discomfort of the emotional and physical varieties around a man, Navarro," she said. "You're nice, and I know, in the end, you and your brothers will do right by my sister. I'm not worried about leaving her here. I can tell she's going to be happy. And she's right. I need to go home."

She took a deep breath and he could see she was calming herself. "Nina, before you decide, listen," Navarro said. "Or maybe 'see' is the appropriate verb." Hating to do it, he pulled out the Lonely Hearts Station newspaper to show her Marvella's advertisement.

"I don't understand," Nina said.

"The game is simple." He sighed. "It looks like Marvella's planning on using your bed in place of the table normally used for playing a last-one-at-the-table-wins kind of chicken."

He hated the dismayed look on her face. "Usually, the men who participate leave pretty quickly when the bull starts rushing them. The table, chairs, cards, whatever props are used, usually get a bit of a tossing from the bull. But whoever has the grapes to stay the longest, wins. Usually a tough call—money or getting gored." He pondered that for a moment. "Audiences love it."

"You're saying my bed may be damaged."

"Pretty much."

"Can't we stop her?" Nina asked, her face pale.

"You could call her and ask her not to use your bed, but I don't think that would do anything but let her know she's succeeded at upsetting you."

"I'd planned for the movers to get the bed this weekend. I thought Marvella just wanted money." She stared at him. "But she's not after money at all, is she?"

"You are innocent," Navarro said. "Money is a by-product of what she's really after, which is to run her sister out of business, in my opinion. And cause havoc for my family, since we keep lousing up her revenge schemes." He grinned happily. "We do love playing the spoilers."

"I never dreamed of something like this happening."

He took her hand in his, then gently pulled her against his chest. "You are innocent," he repeated.

Her heart began beating hard at the intense look in his eyes. "Not experienced with crazy women, maybe."

"We need a plan," Navarro said, "for getting that bed back."

His thumb stroked her cheek. Nina felt herself melting. "I don't see splintered remains in that bed's future."

"Wouldn't do much for its charm," Navarro agreed. He moved his thumb to her throat.

Nina shivered. "Maybe the charm is just a superstition."

"Charms always are. That's where their romance lies."

"It hurts," Nina said, "to envision our family bed crushed by bulls, all its charm kicked to pieces. I always imagined I'd get pregnant in that bed."

Navarro cleared his throat, visions of him getting a naked Nina very pregnant in that bed all too pleasant. He shook himself. "There is some fine print," he said reluctantly. "But it's very fine."

"What does it say?" She peered at the paper. "Oh. Winner wins the bed, the prize purse and the dates." Her eyes got big as she looked up at Navarro. "I'm going to enter myself. Not for the dates, of course."

"No," Navarro said, shocked. "You are not going to sit in a bed while a bull dashes at you with deathly intent. You're terrified of *horses*."

"I will enter," Nina said. "It's my bed, and I *will* save it."

He felt all the sexual appetite drain out of him as fear rushed in. Nina was just nutty enough to do it. "Nina, you are a guest in my home. I will not let you get stomped."

"I'll do it," Last said, walking into the room. "I have little left to live for."

Navarro stared at his little brother's outrageous hair. Dyed blond, it stuck straight up from his head in a chicken-wing style, the sides shaved to contribute to the punk-rock effect.

There was a small gold hoop pierced through his left ear.

"Holy smokes," Navarro said. "You look like David Bowie. What happened?"

"I was drunk and—"

Nina stiffened. "It doesn't matter now. Thank you for your offer, Last. But it won't be necessary. I can take care of myself. No heroics are necessary to save my sister or me." She eyed him with distaste. "I don't know what Valentine saw in you."

Navarro whirled to stare at Nina. "Hey!"

She raised her brows at him. "Hey, yourself. No wonder you guys live at Malfunction Junction. Quite frankly, Valentine and I have had enough of that in our lives." She headed out of the kitchen.

"Wait!" Navarro sent Last an annoyed glance as he went after Nina. He caught her hand, pulling her to face him. "No stomping off. We were in the middle of something good before Bowie freaked me out."

"I don't like him," Nina said. "He thinks only of himself."

"Well, that is true," Navarro mused. "But I can't slap sense into his head, though I'd like to."

"My sister is having a baby," Nina snapped. "He doesn't have to run around acting like he's doing all the work. She's the one tossing her crackers every morning."

Navarro hesitated. "Does she?"

"Yes, damn it," Nina said with heat.

"She couldn't get to a hairdresser to dye her hair in a blond cockatoo if she wanted. And he does have something to live for. He has a *child*."

Navarro nodded. "Nina, I know all this. Let's not let this involve us, okay? Family screws everything up."

"Not for me, it doesn't." Nina stared up at him. "I love my sister. I'm going to stay out of her business, but I'm also going to look out for her. Frankly, I don't think Last's fit to be a father to a child. Maybe none of you are."

How could he disassociate himself from his family? It was impossible. They were a wagon wheel full of broken spokes.

But they were a wheel that rolled along over life's ruts.

"Last's an idiot," Navarro said. "He should be flash-frozen until he ages to maturity." He was still holding Nina's hand, and she hadn't pulled away, so he decided to roll with it. "I'm sorry Valentine's not feeling well," he said. "Maybe Doc should look at her."

"What does a man know about a woman's body?" she said with a light sniff that spoke of incoming tears. He overlooked the comment.

"We know nothing," Navarro said. "That's what makes us irresistible boneheads."

She sniffed against his shirtfront. But she didn't slap him, and he figured he was on a winning course.

"Well, we know how to make a woman feel good," he said, trapping her with a laugh when she tried to pull away from him. "Hey, librarian. Maybe you should show me how to read."

"You read just fine. You read that ad."

"Yes, but maybe what I want to learn now is body language."

"Mine would be telling you to buzz off," she said, moving from his arms.

"And I would pretend not to understand," Navarro said.

"No surprise, I guess." But the memory of Mimi's words about Jefferson love knocked the cold edge from her voice.

Mimi had seemed quite sincere about the fact that Jefferson males were worth the pain.

"I have a plan," Navarro said. "Actually,

I have two. Just so you know, so that you'll be tempted to continue talking to me. You know you want to."

She turned her back to him and stirred the soup.

"Nina," he said softly, his breath at the nape of her neck making her shiver. "Trust me." He turned her to face him. Having to look into his eyes and see her darkest fears mirrored there was painful, but he didn't let go of her arms.

"Trust me," he repeated.

I don't know if I can trust anyone, she thought.

And trusting a Jefferson didn't seem like a particularly good idea, despite Mimi's warning. Especially this one. There was a laundry list of reasons not to like this man or to trust him or to fall for him. There was the baby that he considered his family's alone—maybe he was romancing her because of that. Navarro was too smooth and suave—maybe a trait of cowboys with sexy, one-dimensional hearts. And the family itself was reputed to be wild. Malfunctioning.

Surely she risked the one part of her she

held most cloistered—her heart—if she allowed herself to fall for this man's considerable charm.

"Give me one good reason," she whispered.

He nodded. "I will."

And then his mouth claimed hers until Nina realized that the last thing she ever wanted to do was to distrust this man who was stealing her librarian's sanity.

She took a deep breath as they pulled apart, trying to still her racing heart. And then reality came racing back.

"Excuse me," Crockett said. "Navarro, dude, Marvella's on the phone for you."

Chapter Seven

"The witch will pay," Navarro muttered. "She messed up an entirely wonderful kiss." He looked at Nina sorrowfully. "Just when I had you right where I wanted you."

"Where was that?"

"Convinced." He went to grab the phone from his brother. "Marvella asked for me, specifically?"

"Yeah. Something to do with the bed."

Navarro grimaced. "Hello?"

"Navarro Jefferson?"

"Speaking." He looked at Nina, who had turned pale. He couldn't blame her. As he well knew, the bed had her dreams and her memories represented in its delicate wood frame.

"This is Marvella, owner of—"

"I know who you are," he interrupted.

"How can I be of service?" *Cut to the chase,* he thought. *We're all ready to quit hanging off the cliff.*

"Service is exactly why I called. I've run an ad for a rodeo game called Cowboy Bed Check. Very inventive, I believe. Possibly very profitable."

Rodeo crowds loved amusements and diversions. He'd have to bet Marvella was right—the witch. "I saw the ad."

"Excellent. Then I'm reaching some of my target market," she said. "Cowboys. So, I think it would behoove all of us if you entered. I'll bet you could win Valentine's bed back for her."

He raised his brows. "What's the catch?"

"Catch?" Marvella repeated. "Why would there be a catch?"

"I'm just assuming there is one, or you'd just give Nina and Valentine their bed back."

She clicked her tongue into the phone. "No employer lets an employee leave owing wages, sir. I'm sure you would not have a profitable ranch if everyone knew that working for the Jeffersons meant they could run off with advance monies owing."

"How much do you want for the bed?" he demanded, his gaze on Nina's round eyes.

"No, I don't want money. The event itself is an attraction, which will bring customers who will pay for food and drink... and other things. What I need now are participants," she said silkily. "That's why I called."

"How many participants?" Maybe if he loaded the bed with his brothers, they could somehow save the bed and return it to its rightful owner. "We have a large family."

"Just you," Marvella cooed. "After all, if I have too many Jeffersons in one event, it becomes a circus, with the ladies and all."

"Exactly what you're looking for."

"Well, yes, but the drama is so much more intense if you were inspired to stay on the bed the longest. To be a hero, of course. For Nina's sake." She laughed. "I saw you two kissing on the street yesterday. My, it makes a woman wish for younger days."

"You're weird," Navarro said. "And you make my skin crawl."

She hung up in his ear.

"Crap," Navarro said. "Honesty is not always the best policy."

Nina stared at him. Navarro took a deep breath. "Maybe I'm not good at negotiating with crazy women. I probably should have studied more in Abnormal Psych class. I'm sorry."

She shook her head. "It's okay."

But it wasn't. And he knew it. His gut turned inside out. "I should have kept my mouth shut and played her line a little longer. Good fishermen know how to do that."

"She'll call back," Crockett said. He stood by the wall, picking his fingernails with a huge knife.

"Why do you think so?" Navarro asked.

"She's addicted to power. She thinks she's holding all the cards."

Nina looked from one twin to the other. "She'd be happy if I entered. Don't you think?"

"Absolutely not," both twins said at once.

"Totally wouldn't interest her," Navarro said.

"Not a bit," Crockett seconded. "She's

looking for muscles to display to the ladies."

"Muscles," Nina echoed. "I guess so."

"Don't worry," Navarro said. "Between all the heads in this family, we'll figure it out."

Crockett grinned. "You're scaring Nina."

Navarro held his ground, staring at the woman in front of him. All he wanted to do was to kiss her. He wanted to tell her he'd buy her a thousand beds, even though he really didn't care if they *ever* had a bed. All this talk about *beds* was driving him insane.

She blinked at him, looking like a little librarian lost in the book stacks, and his heart melted. Darn her Mrs. Piggle-Wiggle heart. She was no more wearing white granny panties that stretched to the third rib than he was mining gold in Alaska.

He couldn't stop thinking about what she *was* wearing. A silly grin stretched across his face as he looked at her, all soft and round and peachy and kind of nervous as she stared at him.

"Don't you worry about a thing," Navarro told her.

She smiled, her lips quivering. His heart dropped somewhere below his belt.

Here we go. I've totally lost my mind over this woman—and it's the worst thing I could have let happen.

AN HOUR LATER, Crockett and Navarro and Last sat in the barn, debating their strategy.

"I say we steal it," Last said.

"No one's listening to you," Crockett said. "You have scary hair and an earring. We can't trust you to have a sane suggestion."

"I was drunk," Last said. "It's not like I did it in a moment of rational thought."

"Precisely," Navarro said, "and it's got to stop. The drinking ends now. You were soaked the night you got Valentine pregnant—"

"I don't think I did it," Last said. "Remember, I already told you that."

Crockett rolled his eyes.

"And," Navarro continued, "I found you in the bushes the other night, loaded off your feet. Today, you come in looking like a freak-show attraction. Bro, the insanity circus is folding up its tent today. Out of biz. *Comprendes?*"

Last looked at his two brothers sorrowfully. "I don't have a drinking problem."

"Maybe yes, maybe no. What you have is a major pity party problem, and I vote you snap out of it," Navarro said.

"Before we snap you out of it," Crockett said agreeably. "Lotta work needs to be done around here. You don't want to be here, you go next door and help Mimi look after the sheriff. Or you go fix fence. But this family pulls together. We're inviting you to do your share—or you'll have to check out of the hotel."

Last went pale. "You'd kick me out?"

Navarro nodded. "We love you, Last. You've always been the weight that kept us balanced. God knows we've relied on you. Sometimes, it was your rose-colored glasses that kept us trying to live right, for your sake. We wanted to live up to what you remembered about the family and what you dreamed of for a family." He took a deep breath. "But now it's time for us to take back the reins. You're in trouble. We all need to face it. Whether or not Valentine is bearing your child is incidental. All that will be settled later. The important fact is that you got involved in a situation that could have bankrupted the ranch."

A tear spilled from one of Last's eyes. "I know."

"And you harmed someone else's life by being careless. If Valentine is having your baby, you bear half responsibility for the way it happened. No one goes out in the rain without a raincoat, dude," Crockett said. "As you've preached to us many times over the years."

"I'm so ashamed," Last said. "The last thing I ever wanted to do was let y'all down."

"Don't let us down more by mistreating Valentine," Navarro said. "She doesn't deserve it. And you should have more respect for yourself."

"No more drinking," Crockett said sternly. "We love you, but from this day forward, you face your problems head-on."

"Okay," Last said. "Okay."

"Good," Navarro said. "Now, go get that mess of hair buzzed off your head."

"Earring comes out, too," Crockett said. "Today. If Mason saw you—"

"I know, I know," Last said hurriedly. He jumped up from his chair and left the barn.

Crockett looked at Navarro. "What do you think?"

Navarro shook his head. "My mind can no longer absorb the shock where Last is concerned."

Crockett sighed. "So, what about Cowboy Bed Check?"

Navarro closed his eyes for a second. "I suppose Marvella wants me to call her back and plead for an entry form."

"Sure she does. Feeds her power."

"Do we have an alternative idea?" Navarro asked. "I swear, I'm not keen on this plan. It feels disastrous."

Crockett drummed on the wooden barrel they sat around. "We steal it."

Navarro focused his attention on his twin. "You know, I could hear you thinking about agreeing with Last's nefarious thought."

"It's a twin thing. That uber-connection you and I are supposed to have."

"Like when we burned down Shoeshine

Johnson's barn by accident. My mind was telling me that an old barn goes up fast, but your mind was telling me that I could put the fire out."

"Exactly. And your mind was saying run and mine was saying use the stall shower hose as a fire extinguisher." Crockett grinned. "I told you that crazy old man stored illegal fireworks in his barn. You didn't want to believe me."

"Still, it wasn't worth the hiding we got from the sheriff," Navarro said. "Even if those were great fireworks for December."

Crockett laughed. "We can do anything."

"Yeah. They called us the Twin Lanterns for months after we knocked over his old kerosene lamp." Navarro kicked his boots up on a wood rail, starting to feel better. "Twin Lanterns. I guess we can do anything. Just not anything *right*. I don't know if I'm up for stealing."

"You'd rather compete than steal the bed." Crockett mused. "I could go in your place."

"What's her angle?" Navarro asked. "I thought she'd jump at all of us going to the rodeo."

"'Cause then we'd win, and anyway, she can't trust us when we all get together. We're just as likely to run out of there with the bed, like little ants scurrying away with a cracker crumb on our backs." Crockett flicked an ant off the rail. "Start over, little guy," he told the ant.

Navarro stared at his brother. "That's it," he said, suddenly hit by inspiration. "I'm going to start this whole thing over."

"Great," Crockett said. "I always like to relive the past. Repeat my mistakes. Enjoy the agony of defeat."

"Yes," Navarro said. *"Precisely."*

NINA HESITATED, LISTENING to the sound of something rattling against the window-pane. Frowning, she realized someone was hitting the windowpane. She pulled back the curtain and shook her head at Navarro down below.

"It's your house," she said after opening the window. "Did you forget where the front door was? Need a rescue party?"

"We weren't through talking," Navarro told her, "when I had to take the call from the witch of Lonely Hearts Station. And I can talk to you from here, because I gave my house to you." He grinned.

"You're sneaky," Nina told him. "Don't waste it on me. I recognize a charm offensive when I see it."

"Are you inviting me in?"

She shook her head at him. "Never."

"Okay, then you'll have to hear me out from here. First, I need to talk to you about the two plans I mentioned earlier, before we were interrupted. Second, I need—"

"Is this going to take long? Because I think my sister is trying to sleep."

"Well, we have to talk. Talking is important," Navarro said. "Women love to hash things out. I'm trying it your way, the female way. 'Let's talk,' I said to myself tonight. But I had no one to talk to about our situation."

"Our situation?" Nina tried not to let him sway her.

"Yes, our situation. Yours and mine. Our fortunes are woven together by a bed, one might say. And a baby. So we should talk."

"I was going to sleep," Nina said, not trusting his mood.

"In my bed?" Navarro asked.

Nina turned to glance around the room. "We didn't debate whose room was whose. We just settled in. Is this your room?"

He grinned. "I believe it is. And it's a very comfy bed, isn't it?"

"A bit oversize, perhaps," Nina said. "But just right for a big man, I guess. Can we get back to whatever you came for? The two plans?"

"Yes." He took off his hat, staring up at her earnestly. "Nina, I don't think you should return to Dannon. You need to stay here and fight for your bed personally."

"O-kay," Nina said, drawing the word out to illustrate her lack of enthusiasm. "And the other plan?"

"You and I should find the bed. And sleep in it," he said grandly.

Nina's mouth fell open. "To what end?"

"Marking our territory. We chain ourselves to the bed, and Marvella can't move it to the arena to let the bull bash it to pieces."

In some kooky way, Navarro's plan might have merit. Nina stared down at him, thinking. "I don't know if I can chain myself into a bed with a man," she said slowly. "It sounds kind of kinky for me, since I've never been in bed with a man at all. And then what? Even if we're chained to the bed and they can't move it, how do I reestablish possession of it?"

Navarro raised a fist. "We let her know that we're not to be trifled with. Possession is nine-tenths of the law—and we're taking over possession with our nude bodies."

"*Nude?* I don't think so!"

"Can't blame a man for trying."

She rolled her eyes. "Look, I think you may be a little off center with your idea, but you may be getting close to something good. You should come inside so we can talk without making enough noise to wake Valentine. Goodness knows, she doesn't get much sleep with the morning sick— What are you doing?"

He hand-over-handed up a rope and into the tree, then walked across a branch to vault into her window. "Coming to talk to you," he said with a grin. "Much more dramatic than using my keys to open the front door."

She backed up a few steps. "You looked like a monkey!"

"I learned a lot from Curious George." He settled himself into the wing-backed chair in his room with a contented sigh. "I miss my chair. It's my happy zone. Kind of like your bed, I guess."

"Would you fight for your chair?" Nina asked.

"Depends on who wanted it. My brother, yes. You, no. If you wanted to sit in my chair, I'd polish it for you and then I'd always treasure the knowledge that your fanny had sat here. *Have* you sat in my chair?" he demanded hopefully.

"You'll have to be happy with me sleeping in your bed," Nina said, "And I'd like to do it soon."

"That makes two of us, but," he said hurriedly, seeing the look on her face, "I suppose tonight is for strategic planning only."

"Yes," she said firmly.

"Great gown, though." He eyed her knee-length T-shirt with enthusiasm. It read Feed Your Mind A Book and Navarro's glance caught on the letters that were, Nina realized uncomfortably, right above her bosom.

"I'm hungry," he said.

"Can we move on with the plans?" Nina demanded. She grabbed a fluffy white robe from her suitcase.

"You haven't unpacked yet?" he asked, his tone disappointed.

"I'm not staying long enough."

"As I mentioned." He stared at her. "I'll miss you if you go. For a librarian, you have a totally crazy effect on me. I *like* it. Definitely worth giving up my favorite chair."

Nina sighed. "Thanks. I guess." He made her crazy, too, but in so many ways she wasn't sure if the manic energy was positive or not.

"What did you mean, you'd never been in bed with a man before?" Navarro asked. "Not that I'm trying to get personal or anything."

Nina felt herself blush. "I didn't mean that quite the way it sounded," she said.

"Feel free to expound."

"No, thanks." She glared at him.

He grinned. "Can't blame a guy for trying."

"Yes, I can," Nina said with heat. "That's the problem with you boys. You all think you shouldn't be blamed for being emotional escape artists."

"Hey, I'm the one trying to chain myself to a bed with you," Navarro said, sitting up. "No escape there."

She stared at him. "I just don't want you coming on to me anymore. I have serious things on my mind, and I don't think you're ever serious."

"I do have a dry wit, overlooked by people who don't know me well. Maybe serious is not my way, but that doesn't mean I don't feel the same way you do," Navarro said. "Some people laugh when they're in pain."

"Is that what you're doing?" Her blood began a slow, hopeful pounding.

"Now who's getting personal?" His gaze met hers.

She looked down and then forced herself to meet his gaze. "I am."

"Why?"

"Maybe it doesn't matter." She gave him a defiant glare.

Navarro put on his hat. "Let me know when it does."

And then he left her room the same way

he'd entered—Curious George hanging in a tree.

"Or maybe George of the Jungle," she muttered, spying out the window as he mounted his horse and galloped away.

"You all right in there?" Valentine called, knocking on her bedroom door.

"Come on in," Nina said, closing the window.

"I thought I heard voices. I wouldn't have bothered you, only the voices sounded kind of mad, so I thought you were watching TV. I can't sleep," Valentine said, settling herself into the wing-backed chair. "Mmm, warm seat. Were you sitting here?"

"No," Nina said on a sigh. "Leather must stay warmer than man-made material."

"Maybe." Valentine tucked her feet under her. "Can't you sleep?"

"No." Nina brushed her hair—pretty late to recover her beauty ritual since Navarro had already seen her plain and unready for visitors. But now they'd seen each other without false pretenses and there was no recovering that intimacy, either. "Do you ever wonder what our lives might have been like if that car accident hadn't killed Mom and Dad?"

"No," Valentine said passionately. "I never let myself think about it. I only want to remember the good times."

"Me, too." Nina set the brush down. "Do you really think you can be happy here with the Jeffersons? They have a slightly half-baked streak to them."

"I know." Valentine shrugged. "They're going to help me find a job. They're going to help me raise my baby, and frankly, I like the idea of a bunch of men being father figures to my child. I didn't plan on a pregnancy, but I'm glad for it, and I'm happy that my life is starting over. In some strange way, this baby birthed *me*."

Nina nodded. "All right. I accept that, and I'm thrilled you're happy."

"And so what about you?"

Nina looked toward the tree outside the window. "I'd never fit in here. I'm afraid of horses. I don't particularly like the ranch. I'm not keen on all the brothers. It's not for me, I suppose, but you and I were always opposite sides of the same coin. In a good way."

"You like Navarro."

"I don't." Nina shook her head. "I feel alarmed around him, excited, upset, nervous, angry—"

"Nina, you may be falling in love," Valentine said. "I know the signs aren't logical to a brain that thrives on order, but it might be worth redefining your concept of love."

"It's sexual. I'm positive. On both our parts. And that's not love," Nina said with a sigh.

"Have you slept with Navarro?"

"No!"

Valentine giggled. "Then how is it sexual?"

"I don't know! I just think it is. He's obsessed with my underwear and I…I'm obsessed with keeping it on around him." Nina glanced toward the window, wanting reassurance that Navarro wasn't lurking in the tree. "I think that if he didn't make me feel so many emotions at once, I could pick one, settle on it and disrobe."

"Nina! What are you talking about?" Valentine's face was lit with merriment. "Disrobe?"

"I'm just saying that if I knew whether

it was love or not, I might be able to undress for him." Nina felt guilty even saying such a thing to her little sister. "If I knew I was in love with him, I could enjoy making love with him. If I could tell I wasn't in love with him, I could indulge in a little affair I'd never forget. But since I feel so many things when I'm around him, I just get confused and give up."

Valentine laughed. "Sister, what a dilemma."

"Tell me about it," Nina said crossly. "My hormones are moving at light-speed, and it's making me cranky."

"'Nina and Navarro' has a cute ring to it."

Nina winced. "Baby sister, run along to your room. It's lights out for me. I've got to pack some things and plot."

"Why are you leaving?" Valentine said. "I need you here."

"I've got a job. And you have more than enough people around you, ready to make your life easy."

"But I want you. I want the time we never got to spend together," Valentine said. "Does Navarro know you're leaving?"

"Yes, but he mainly offered to chain himself to the heirloom bed with me, and I don't know that there was much of a Casablanca goodbye in that." Nina shook her head, examining a scratch on her arm left from when the horse had tossed her. "He's just not a man that can be understood or predicted. And that's not good for my stability."

Valentine got up, swishing to the door in her long gown and robe. "You've been searching for stability all your life. Maybe it's time to give something else a try."

"Chaos and disorder make for anarchy," Nina said. "I'm a safety player at heart."

"Maybe I should have been," Valentine said. "But I'm glad I'm not. Kinda weird that I'm so happy about my circumstances, isn't it?"

"No," Nina said, thinking, *I'd love a baby. That's why I was willing to let a bull rush at me to win back my bed. And Navarro is definitely the survival-of-the-fittest kind of male any woman would choose to father her offspring.*

Of course, he didn't want children, but then, he wasn't The One for her, either. And she didn't need that handsome cowboy riding to her rescue. She was nothing if not sensible. She could rescue herself.

"I'm going to change my flight reservations and figure out how to dress up like a cowboy," Nina said. "I'm going to enter that Cowboy Bed Check and be the last one sitting on the bed." She gave Valentine a determined look. "I'm getting my charmed bed *back*."

Valentine gasped. "Navarro's going to kill you when he finds out! If the bull doesn't get you first."

"I don't care." Nina looked at her sister's softly rounded stomach. *To him, the bed was just another adventure.*

But to Nina, the bed represented family—past, present and future.

"I'm not going to lose it," she said. "It's *ours*."

Chapter Eight

Nina didn't see Navarro at all on Friday, which was annoying because he thought her plane was leaving on Saturday. He didn't know she'd changed her flight plans, so he should have dropped by to say good-bye, at least.

She didn't want to examine why her feelings were hurt.

But at five o'clock, when he came riding up on Curious George while she and Valentine were sitting on the porch sipping tea, Nina's soul jumped for joy.

"Howdy, ladies," he said, tipping his hat.

"Hi, Navarro," Valentine said with a sweet smile. "How are you?"

His eyes stayed on Nina as he answered. "Good."

An awkward pause settled over them.

Nina wasn't going to say a word. After all, he was the one who'd gotten miffed and exited her window.

"I owe you an apology," he finally said to Nina.

"Well, I think I hear the teakettle whistling," Valentine said brightly. "Why don't I go see if it is?"

He waited until she'd left. "Nina," he said, "you're driving me insane."

She nodded. "Likewise. Is that the preface or the ending to your apology?"

"It's the general state of confusion I'm suffering. I've never known a woman who could tie me up in knots the way you do, and yet I know the possibility of a relationship with you is nonexistent. I do believe you'd kill me."

"You could be right. Though it will remain a mystery."

He sighed. "I had to meet the only librarian who didn't follow the stereotype."

"I had to meet a cowboy who didn't live up to the stereotype," she said softly.

"I do!" he protested. "I'm handsome, hardworking, handsome—"

"Well, you certainly have yourself convinced."

His gaze touched her white linen dress and her bare feet. "You look very pretty."

She wasn't about to tell him he looked handsome after he'd just told her twice how handsome he was. What a compliment-fisher! "How's Curious George?"

"Still sorry he threw you the other night."

She shrugged. "Can't trust a male."

"Actually this is a—never mind," he said with a sigh. "I suppose all Curious George is to you is a giant chocolate-colored horse, not the dark bay Thoroughbred he actually is."

"No, but, if it helps at all, he really didn't hurt me. I think I slid over his neck. I don't think he actually tossed me. And it was more my fault than his, if I were to be honest."

He patted the horse's neck. "Still. He is trained to handle just about anything. He should have been able to behave for one untrained rider."

"He doesn't know me very well." She

reached up to rub the horse's nose that he'd stuck over the railing.

"I don't, either," Navarro said. "But I wouldn't throw you over."

Her gaze flew to his. Her blood started tickling right before she felt a rush of wish-fulness. "I'm sorry," she said, "I know there's some feeling between us. But it's not what it needs to be. I think we both know that."

He swallowed. "I know you're right. I just haven't completely convinced myself. It's a brain/heart ratio thing that's out of whack inside me."

She nodded. "I know."

"I cussed Last for not being able to make rational choices. But now I'm the one who's not feeling too rational." Gripping the reins tighter in his hand, he glanced at the leather winding over his fingers. "Nina, I knew the first time I laid eyes on you that you were a different kind of woman. I wish I had time to figure you out."

"What's the fun in that?" Nina said lightly.

"My mind likes puzzles. And you make me curious."

She smiled and rubbed the horse's nose one more time. "You *and* your horse."

"Yeah." He nodded. "So I guess I really came to say goodbye."

She waited, her heart stuck in a dull rhythm, a clock that needed winding to tick fast again.

"Do you need a ride to the airport?"

"No," she said, not mentioning her canceled plans. "No, thank you. A cab would be better."

It wasn't exactly a lie. She hadn't said she was actually taking one.

"Okay. By the way, I did enter the rodeo."

"You did?"

He nodded, his expression serious. "If I can win your bed back for you tomorrow, I will, Nina."

"I didn't think you'd enter," she said, hesitating. It was on the tip of her tongue to say she'd entered under a false name, but maybe he wouldn't recognize her. They wouldn't be in there long, not with a bull rushing at them.

She felt guilty, knowing that she was

going to beat him. "Navarro, don't do it," she said. "It's not that important."

"It is important."

"No, it's really not," she said, her words speeding up as she realized just how much he was risking for her. "It's just a bed."

"It's your bed. And your charm. And I see it as your honor," he told her seriously.

"You could get hurt!"

"I've gotten away from many bulls in my lifetime. I'll be fine."

He was handsome, Nina acknowledged, wishing he wasn't so aware of it. And cocky.

Brave. And kind.

And her heart knew it.

She couldn't tell him that she intended to win her own history and dreams back. He wouldn't let her do it—but she didn't want to owe him anything. She thought about Valentine, pregnant by a man who didn't want her, and knew she had to take charge of her own destiny.

"Don't do it," she told Navarro. "You won't win."

He grinned. "Our family reputation is that we're wild winners."

She stood, brushing the wrinkles out of her white linen dress because she couldn't meet his gaze. "Goodbye, Navarro," she said. "Call me if Valentine needs me. She doesn't always phone home when she's in trouble."

"I think she's on the upswing," Navarro said easily. "And there isn't much trouble to get into out here, anyway. But I'll keep an eye on her for you."

"Thanks." Nina turned to go inside.

"Nina."

She turned her head to look over her shoulder. "Yes?" Her heart was beating madly inside her.

He looked at her for a long moment, then shook his head. "Nothing. Happy trails."

"You, too."

She went inside and closed the door, wishing it was as easy to close the door on her heart.

"Just heard from Mimi about the sheriff," Crockett said when Navarro rode up to the house. "She says her dad's doing better. He's had a string of good days."

"Glad to hear that."

"She's thinking about running for his office."

Navarro nodded at Crockett. "She could do it."

"Yeah. Helga wants to know if you want meat loaf sent over for dinner."

He wasn't hungry, but Helga's meat loaf was actually pretty good. "I imagine the boys would appreciate that."

"So, where ya been?" Crockett asked. "Your face looks like your heart's quit pumping."

"Thanks, bro. I appreciate your diagnosis." Navarro swung down from the saddle and tied the reins to the porch rail. "Planning to get your medical degree?"

"Hey!" Crockett said. "Don't eat my head, man, I'm not gonna grow another."

"Sorry." Navarro wanted to be alone with his thoughts, mainly the ones about Nina. "I'm all out of parlor conversation, though."

"Hey," Crockett said, following after his brother, "I heard from Frisco Joe and Annabelle. They're fixing to host a large gathering of international wine experts at their vineyard."

"Really? Nice company they're keeping." At least it was good news, he thought.

"And Laredo said he and Katy are studying up a storm. Duke University's really agreeing with him."

"Another studious brother happily biting the dust," Navarro said.

"Yes, intelligent bunch we have here," Crockett said cheerfully. "Ranger sent a postcard from some place in Alaska. He says they're hot on the trail of heart-stopping scenery. Me, I think he and Hannah are just having a blast on the endless road trip."

"Whatever excuse works."

"And," Crockett said, "I got a text message from Tex. So I guess that would be a Tex-message."

He laughed and Navarro gave him an impatient eyeing. "And?"

"He and Cissy are pit-stopped on the banks of the Gulf, eating great seafood and hosting celebrities and other vacationers on their boat. What a life. Nothing to do but float—"

"Bro, I gotta go. Are you done?"

"I guess I am, unless you want to hear about Fannin's e-mail—"

"No." Navarro shook his head. "You're going to say that the tiny red teacup poodle Joy sleeps in his hat, and the flame is never-ending between he and Kelly. And that they sent another e-mail to Helga, saying that life with twins in Ireland is fulfilling."

"Well, not in so many words, but Joy does sleep in his hat—"

"See ya later, bro," Navarro said, closing the door to his makeshift sleeping room in Crockett's face. Too many brothers had bailed from the ranch. Navarro slumped onto the sofa, flipping the TV on while he let his thoughts roam.

Dannon, Delaware, would never be his kind of town. He belonged here, on the ranch. Valentine was happy to move to Union Junction, Texas. Why not her sister?

Valentine was having a Jefferson baby and Nina was not.

Nina wanted babies.

Navarro wanted nothing of the kind.

There was nothing to draw them together for life. "Why am I thinking about forever?" he asked himself. "Life is too complicated to think about long hauls."

Shoot, the brothers couldn't make it a day without hitting one of life's cattle guards. He really had nothing to offer a librarian, unless she simply wanted a cowboy fantasy.

Fantasies he could do.

"Hey!" Crockett pounded on the door. "Forgot to tell you something."

"Come in," Navarro said crossly. "It better be good."

"Last took out his earring and shaved his head. He looks like an egg, but at least the Bowie period is over."

Navarro grunted. "Has he gone to talk to Valentine?"

"I don't think so."

"Then he hasn't come around yet. We need to lock up the liquor cabinet and stow the beer. Replace it with soda and water bottles."

"He can buy his own liquor if he wants, Navarro. No use padlocking the rest of us."

"Out of sight, out of mind, hopefully." Unfortunately, he didn't think that would work for his thoughts about Nina. He just might have a rare case of emotional attachment disturbing his reasoning.

"Have you ever watched these shows?" Crockett asked, flipping to a channel featuring mud wrestling. Two bikini-clad blondes wrestled in the mud, cheered on by a delirious crowd. "They're twins."

"Fancy that," Navarro said, annoyed.

"Ever have a twin fantasy?"

Navarro blinked. "I think I was always more partial to nurse fantasies."

Crockett guffawed. "Yeah?"

"Yeah. Remember how Mimi's mom used to watch a soap while she ironed? 'General Hospital' or something. I guess that's where she got the itch for Hollywood."

"Wonder what happened to her?"

Navarro shook his head. "Just know she wasn't cut out to be a ranch wife."

"It's not easy," Crockett said stoically. "I could go for twins."

"Not me." Navarro switched off the TV. "I'm a one-woman man." He pulled his hat over his face and kicked his boots up on the sofa. "Helluva thing to be."

"Hey, is there something we should discuss?" Crockett asked. "You okay?"

"I'm fine." After a moment of pondering the inside of his hat brim, he said, "I entered the Cowboy Bed Check contest."

"Excellent. Shall I bring a shovel to carry you home in?"

"I'll be all right."

"Yeah. You will."

"I'll be better if I win."

"That's true," Crockett said. "I'll drive you over and back, okay? That way if you're piecemeal, you won't have to bleed out in a taxi."

"You are so much help. A comfort and a reason for faith."

"You're welcome. Get some rest. You're going to need it for the sheer fight-or-flight adrenaline that's going to hit you tomorrow."

"I'm already feeling it."

"Eh, I think that's from Nina leaving town, bro," Crockett said quietly. "Did you ever think about laying all your cards on the table? Instead of getting laid low by the curse of the broken body parts?"

Navarro chose not to answer and closed

his eyes. Crockett left the room, his boots sounding on the stairs.

"I thought about it," Navarro muttered, "I just don't know which cards would win that woman."

"And then there's the trust factor," Crockett called up the stairs. "I don't think either of you really trusts the other. Impossible situation, that."

Navarro groaned. "And then there are days when leaving the ranch behind has some *serious* appeal."

BY NIGHTFALL Nina worried that her sister was putting on a brave face. Last had showed up on the porch, hat in hand, head newly shaved, and asked Valentine out to walk with him.

She did, much to Nina's chagrin. Craning her head out of Navarro's bedroom window, she watched the two people who barely knew each other walk up the road. They weren't walking close to each other, but they weren't walking far apart, either. Just enough distance for comfort between them.

"Could be a turn for the better," Nina

sighed. She snuggled up in the wing-backed chair and thought about not ever seeing this room again after she won her bed back tomorrow. She'd moved her flight and packed her bags.

A knock sounded on the front door. Nina went downstairs, surprised to see a horseless Navarro on the porch. "Hi."

He nodded. "Can I come in?"

She stepped back so he could enter.

"Crockett says we don't trust each other."

"He's probably right." Nina nodded. "But that's not altogether a bad thing. Is it? We don't know each other all that well."

"I feel like I know you better than any woman I've ever met." Navarro tossed his hat onto a chair. "I like you, Nina."

Her eyes widened. "I like you, too. It surprises me, but it's true."

"If all things were equal—if you lived here and I wasn't Last's brother—do you think we'd be more than friends?"

His serious expression stunned her. Nina turned away from him, thinking. "I don't know," she said finally. "We're very different. I'm used to being on my own.

I like my life the way it is. Being more than friends with you would require lots of change on my part."

"And mine." He turned her toward him. "I'd have to learn not to be so stubborn. You require finesse, and autocratic just doesn't cut it."

"You're right."

"Then again, there are parts of me I just can't help, and one of them is wanting to say goodbye this way." He kissed her hard, passionately, and Nina felt her knees buckle.

When he pulled away, she was clutching his arms. "Do that again," she said. He did, and in that moment Nina realized she could kiss him all night. Maybe for two nights. "Oh, no," she murmured. "I could do this forever."

"Don't leave," he said, sweeping her into his arms. "Stay here and get to know me better."

"Maybe I will," she said, knowing she couldn't but wishing she could. "Where are you taking me?" she asked as he carried her up the stairs.

"I'm going to conduct an experiment," he said. "Skank versus Uptight Librarian."

"How will you read the results? There's no control group to test against."

He set her on his bed. "I won't need it. I'll know everything I need to know in an hour or two."

"Mmm. Fast experiment."

He kissed every fingertip on her hand. "Not really. Now see, I figure if you were a skank your fantasy would involve some studded leather. But you're soft," he said, kissing her neck as he lay her back against the pillows. Her blood raced as he kissed along her collarbone. "And you're sweet here," he said, caressing her knees where the T-shirt and robe ended. "You don't feel like a skank."

She smiled. "You're driving me insane. I can't play word games and focus on what you're doing to me."

Stroking her hair away from her face, he said, "You may be the sweetest woman I ever met."

"Well, then this must be my librarian-gone-wild fantasy," Nina whispered. "I'm going to try to be brave here, so don't laugh, because this is all new for me." She took a deep breath. "Navarro, would you like to satisfy your curiosity about my panties?"

He looked as though he'd been granted a wish. Slowly, never taking his eyes off hers, he pushed her gown and robe up. Nina could feel the breeze across her thighs from the open window, and Navarro's rough fingertips trembled against her skin.

"Dare I look?" he asked.

"I don't know. Do you?"

His gaze slowly broke from hers to travel the length of her body. "Black," he said with some surprise. "Black lace. I would never have guessed."

She laughed. "Librarians and basic black? Wouldn't that be a no-brainer? So serviceable, so—"

"Nina, be quiet," Navarro said, reaching to kiss her hard again. "You drive me mad every time you sass me with those plump lips. I told you, it's foreplay for me, all this ladylike defiance, and now I've seen your panties, and I don't think I'll ever be a sane man again."

She tugged him out of his shirt. "I'm willing to be beyond reason for a night."

"Tell me you want this. Tell me I'm not seducing you against your will," Navarro said, removing her robe with great speed. "Breasts like those should be reserved for kings," he said, touching them reverently so that Nina thought she was going to scream if he didn't stop respecting her so much.

"Navarro, this is not against my will. In fact, if you don't get a move on with the cowboy fantasy you've been bragging about, I may have to exit your bed."

"No. No, you're not." He threw his jeans and boots on the floor and crawled in beside her on the bed. "Thank heaven this is my bed, because I want to remember you like this for always. Also, as that is my nightstand, I have condoms in the drawer."

Nina narrowed her eyes at him as he stroked her waist, then her hips and swirled his tongue in her belly button. She nearly cried out from the pleasure of him kissing her hipbones. "Tell me those condoms are not your everyday stash."

He looked up at her. "*Au contraire*. We

get them in our stockings every year at Christmas, courtesy of Last. The little creep."

Nina gasped, "Thank God," as his tongue somehow found a magical place. She arched when he went deeper. "Navarro," she said, pulling him to her. "Kiss me."

He drained her with a searing kiss that left her breathless, and then he put her hand on the part of his body she'd never touched on a man before. "It doesn't feel like it looks in books," she said wonderingly. "It's so much cooler."

"Cooler?" He grinned down at her, his black hair flopping over one eye.

"Yes," Nina said on a moan. "Hard, but soft. Strong, yet—"

"You keep stroking me like that and we're not going to get several hours of pleasure," he said on a growl. His teeth nipped her earlobe, then he kissed her ear.

Nina closed her eyes, then opened them to see Navarro staring down at her. "What is it?" she whispered.

"You're beautiful," he said. "I know many men have probably told you that, but your every feature drives me mad. I have a constant erection around you."

"I never noticed," Nina said with wonder.

"You never looked." He kissed her again, hard.

"Well, I'll be looking from now on, you can be *sure*."

Lightly he tweaked a nipple and Nina gasped with pleasure. "Is it always this much fun?" she asked.

"No, it's always *this* much fun," he said, sliding into her.

Nina cried out at the pain, but Navarro caught her lips with his, kissing her gently as he moved slowly inside her. She held his arms tightly, waiting for the pain to subside, and when it did Nina was amazed by the wonder of the two of them joined as if they were meant to be this way forever. "I love this," she told him. "I love you being inside me."

He stroked her breasts and then between her legs, making her clench tightly around him. Groaning, he said, "Tell me again."

"I love you being inside me."

He stared down into her eyes, holding

himself still as he looked deep into her soul. "You certainly talk dirty for a librarian, and I must say it's refreshing."

She giggled, then her breath caught as he began moving quickly inside her. Passion carried her to a place she couldn't identify. "Stop," she said. "I've got the strangest urge to laugh."

"Go ahead," he told her, plunging deeper. "Laugh all you want. Because I'm going to make sure you do things you never thought you could do."

Comforted by his words, Nina closed her eyes and smiled, but it wasn't laughter that was claiming her; it was spasms of bliss that made her scream with intense pleasure, over and over again. "Oh, my God!" she cried against his shoulder. "Oh, Navarro!"

But he didn't answer this time, his body tensed against hers, every muscle clenched. "You feel wonderful," she told him, raising her legs and circling his waist to pull him against her tighter. He cried out suddenly and Nina held him tight, loving the cowboy he was. *Navarro,* she repeated in her mind, *it was always meant to be Navarro.*

WHEN NINA AWAKENED the next morning, Navarro was gone. A rose and a note lay on the pillow next to hers.

Gone to win back your bed. You're beautiful, and you deserve a man who can give you everything you dream of.

Navarro

Chapter Nine

"Rats!" Nina jumped from her bed. Heroes could be annoying, she decided as she tore through a fast shower. "Love me, leave me, try to impress me by getting gored."

Valentine knocked on the door. "Nina!" she called. "It's time to go!"

"I know. I know!" She hopped into a pair of jeans, debated over which of Navarro's boots to pick out of his closet, finally choosing the dirtiest pair and stuffing two pairs of socks on her feet plus padding in the toe to make them fit. "Come see the cowboy me!"

Valentine walked in, her eyes widening. "What happened to your hair?"

"It's under this hat." Nina pushed down on the handkerchief she'd wrapped around her head and then double-knotted to keep

Navarro's hat on. "He's got a big head, you know. This is harder than I thought it would be. Fortunately, I bought a pair of Wranglers when I hatched this scheme. They are the only things that fit. I had to cut off the shirttail so I wouldn't have ten thousand folds of material in my jeans."

"And still you look like a rather under-nourished cowboy," Valentine said. "Although I must say I'm impressed at how you're hiding your breasts."

"Now that took a bit more work. The poncho was a stroke of genius. Mimi let me borrow hers. Strangely enough, she was all over the scheme and promised not to tell."

"You need a mustache to toughen up your image," Valentine said. "Or a scar."

"Fresh out of the first, and not going to get the second." She turned around. "Do I pass?"

"You certainly don't look like my sister. I'm not even sure you look reputable."

"I know," Nina said impatiently, "but am I manly?"

Valentine blinked. "Was Navarro here last night?"

Nina hesitated. "Why do you ask?"

"Because there's a rose and a note on your pillow."

"Ah." Nina tightened the leather belt with the big shiny buckle around her waist. "Thank goodness I'm no skinny Minnie or this job wouldn't work. Yes, he was here. And then he was gone. Which really annoyed me, because my vision of romance included waking up with the man of my dreams. That part was a fairy tale," she said decisively.

"Nina, are you saying you…made love with Navarro?"

Nina turned to face her sister. "Not in so many words, but if you must know, yes."

"Why?"

Nina blinked. "What do you mean, why?"

Valentine looked uncomfortable. "Nothing good can come of it, you know."

"So nothing was resolved between you and Last? Is that the conclusion I can draw?"

Her sister shook her head. "It has nothing to do with us. We've decided to proceed as separate parties, both interested parties in the well-being of the child."

"That sounds like paperwork," Nina said.

"There'll be some," Valentine admitted. "Mimi's husband will draw up the papers."

"And where do I fit into this?"

"You're the beloved aunt, of course." Valentine touched her sister's arm. "Nina, this baby is going to be fine without you worrying about her. And so am I. Though we love you very much, you're not responsible for us."

Nina blinked back swift tears. "All right."

"What Last and I decided doesn't affect you," Valentine said. "Did you fall in love with Navarro?"

Nina stopped worrying the bandana she was tying around her neck to further disguise any cleavage the poncho might not cover. "All these colors surely confuse the eye."

"Nina." Valentine turned her around. "Are you in love with him?"

"I wasn't looking for love. We just had a mutual fantasy." Nina turned away, not wanting to admit that her heart was far more involved than she was telling.

"It'll be my fault if you've given up your most important treasure," Valentine said sadly. "I brought you here. I could see you were falling for him. I should have insisted you go away, but selfishly I wanted you with me. Nina," she said, her voice cracking. "It's not the bed that is our biggest treasure, it's our self-respect."

"It's all right, Valentine. I didn't do anything I didn't want to do. I wasn't out of my head, and I wasn't seduced. I wanted to be with him, and believe me, it was everything I thought it would be."

"Will you marry him?"

"I don't see that happening." Nina flipped the top of her jeans inside her boots. "We're far too different."

Valentine nodded. "I know."

Nina sighed. "Will you stop worrying? Truly, it was the most wonderful experience of my life, besides Mom bringing you home from the hospital. Calm down. It's not like Navarro tore a hole in my soul. Now, let's go before I miss my greatest moment."

"You're not serious, are you?" Valentine stared at her. "You can't compete against Navarro. If he finds out you did this, especially after last night, I don't think he's going to be too happy."

"I can't think about that. I have to think about getting back what's ours. And if this is how I have to do it, then so be it."

"Was it…everything you hoped your first time would be?"

Nina looked at her sister. "It was that and more. He made me feel like a woman, as corny as that song is."

"But you're dressed like a man! Nina, this is crazy! What will you do if he finds out you're next to him on that bed?"

"He won't," Nina said defiantly. "I'm totally disguised."

"You're wearing his boots and hat."

"Yes, but if you notice, they're just the same as every other ones you see on the street. Plus these are very dusty, so you know he's probably forgotten he has them. And since when do guys notice details, anyway? Especially with a heavy-tonnage animal dashing at them?"

"Nina, if you get hurt, I'll flip out," Valentine warned. "This is my fault from start to finish. It's all going so very wrong. If the two of you had met under different circumstances, without me in the middle causing problems, you might have had a smooth courtship that transitioned into love. As it is, it's too crazy. And I can't bear you getting hurt—either by the bull or Navarro."

"Look." Nina took a deep breath. "Remember when you told me to butt out of your life?"

Valentine nodded.

"Well, now I'm asking you to do the same. I don't need him to fight my battles for me, and I don't want you worrying so much." She lightly touched her sister's cheek. "It's not good for the baby. She'll grow up to be a worrywart. Very ugly, that."

"Someone's got to do the worrying. You've certainly turned reckless since you've been here. I'll get the keys to Navarro's truck," she said with a sigh. "Jefferson must be to blame for all the brave antics going on around here."

Nina hurried out front, halting when she saw Navarro.

"Hello, Miss Nina," he said.

"Oh, Crockett." Nina put a hand over her chest. "You scared me. I thought you were Navarro—wait a minute. What do you mean, Miss Nina? How'd you guess?"

Crockett grinned. "Navarro asked me to keep an eye on his lil' peach. Said you had a penchant for getting into trouble and that he'd found a neat pile of his old clothes stacked in his closet, looking like they were about to go somewhere. Also, when he called Marvella to kiss and make up so he could enter the contest, he asked who he'd be competing against. Marvella said she had an entry form from a cowboy by the name of H. A. Rey of whom she'd never heard. Marvella makes it her business to know about cowboys.

"Now, Miss Nina, you don't think Navarro wouldn't guess what you were up to with that name?" Crockett winked at her. "Well, it was almost a sexual bread crumb, Navarro said, dropped to further entice him. You know how he loves a challenge. He said he was touched you used the name of the author of the Curious George books, almost as if you were daring him to guess your secret." Crockett grinned. "I've never heard of a sexual bread crumb before, but my twin's a bit odd that way."

Nina let out an exasperated breath. "Crockett, you've got to let me compete. It's my bed!"

"Now, no can do. My brother would beat my head in," Crockett said easily, tipping his hat at Valentine. "And it's such a pretty head, I just can't allow that to happen."

"So he set a guard on me," Nina said between clenched teeth.

"Not a guard, Miss Nina. First, he said he removed the truck keys to stymie you. But then he said such a smart card-catalogette with a wily feminine side such as you couldn't be underestimated. There will be no pulling info off the Internet about hot-wiring a truck." Crockett grinned approvingly. "That one I wouldn't have thought of. So he considered pulling out the computer card, but in the interest of fair play and laziness, he just invited me over to visit with you ladies today."

"He is the most annoying man I ever met," Nina said. "Valentine, are you hearing all this?"

Valentine laughed, seating herself next to Crockett on the porch. "Want some lemonade?"

"I would. Thank you," he said kindly, and Nina groaned, realizing her sister's way worked best, cozying up to these men who were stubbornly determined to have their own way.

"After all the trouble I went through," Nina said. "It makes me mad that Navarro outwitted me."

"He's crazy like that," Crockett said. "We all sort of admire that in him."

Nina had to admit, though it went severely against her grain, that she admired it, too. "But we're missing everything! Don't you want to see what happens?"

"What I really want to see is you getting out of that outfit," Crockett said, "before my brother comes home with the hard-won prize for his lady fair. Wouldn't that be a shame if he went to all that trouble and came home to find a *man?*"

"HE DOESN'T LISTEN," Nina said, tossing her suitcases into the taxi while Valentine looked on. For the moment she'd eluded

Crockett by sending him to the big house for some "decent" food for Valentine. The truth was, after Navarro's latest stunt, Nina was more determined than ever to catch her plane and go home to Dannon. "Navarro thinks he's invincible and that little women are ornaments on the fabric of his life."

"You make a pretty ornament," Valentine said, "but I can see it's not exactly your style."

"No, it's not. Now I know why you were always irritated with me trying to do everything for you in 'your best interests.' Feel free to point out this learning experience to me the next time I slip up."

Valentine smiled. "Having you look out for me wasn't all that bad. Sometimes it was really good. Let's face it, Nina, I'm not you. You're far more independent than I am."

Nina closed the door. "Tell Crockett I'm sorry I had to mess up his guard duty. I hope Navarro won't be too mad at him. Be sure he knows it was all my fault."

Valentine frowned. "But what about the bed? What if it he wins it?"

"Call the movers and have them ship it home. They've already got the address since I was planning on winning it myself."

"What if Navarro doesn't win?" Valentine said worriedly. "What if he gets hurt?"

"That's what he gets for trying to be a hero. And a sexist pig." Nina leaned out the car window to kiss her sister goodbye. "I'll miss you. Call me when you're close to your due date. I'll come to be with you if you want me to."

"Of course," Valentine said, starting to sob. "I'll always want you with me."

They hugged tightly again.

"I love you, Nina. You're the best sister anyone could have. I'm so sorry—"

"Shh," Nina said. "No more sorries. You concentrate on my niece or nephew, because, quite frankly, it looks like you'll be having the only baby in the family."

"Nina," Valentine whispered, so the cabdriver couldn't hear. "Call me, okay? Tonight? Tell me you're safe."

"I will," Nina promised. "Goodbye."

Valentine let go of her sister reluctantly. The driver backed the taxi up and drove down the road. Nina held back her tears, then leaned out the window to wave good-bye.

Valentine stood in the road staring after her, her long dress hanging awry at the hem, looking forlorn. Nina sighed, pulling her head back inside and rolling up the window to keep out the Texas dust.

"Babies having babies," the taxi driver said.

Nina shut her eyes. It was the road to paradise that led a woman to take the wrong fork in the road. Once a man loved you, all you could do was follow the call of the wild.

"Thankfully, I'm a common-sense librarian," she said to the back of the taxi driver's bald head. "I may have deviated from the ivory tower, but I'm locked up tight again."

"Whatever," he said. "You young girls think you know it all."

She did. It wasn't the charmed bed that made all things possible; it was a woman's respect for herself.

"Did ya hear about the big rodeo?" the driver asked.

"Just a little," Nina said crossly.

"Heard it got postponed to tonight, on account of the bull getting sick."

"Sick?"

"Yeah. The showcase bull, which was to participate in that wacky Cowboy Bed Check, came down with a case of the runs. Pardon me for saying so, but it was cowpie central, if you know what I mean. Heard the owner was fit to be tied and threatened to make chair covers out of her marquee bull. Guess she was shouting that her sister was up to her old tricks again, but her sister had been out of town. Turned out some kids coming through had tossed a bunch of animal crackers into the pen. Not good for a bull, all that kiddie fiber, I guess."

"Eww." Nina grimaced, then leaned forward to grab the seat back beside the driver. "Does that mean the contest will be tonight?"

"That's what I just said, right? BadAss Blue's owner had to borrow a bull from her sister, of all people. And the replacement bull's the meanest one in Texas. Delilah made Marvella promise that all the proceeds from the bed event go to charity before she lent out her bounty bull—and Marvella has to do ten hours of community service in Lonely Hearts Station. Her sister said Marvella needed to get to know some of the folks who've lost their jobs and some of the families who stay in town despite the hard times. I imagine that stuck in Marvella's craw pretty good," he said with a chuckle. "Ever heard of Bloodthirsty Black?"

"No." Nina thought quickly. She had no disguise. But she also didn't have Crockett shadowing her every move. Valentine would have to admit that Nina had made a clean getaway. They'd be looking for her at the airport.

"Now, Bloodthirsty Black is no ringer," he continued, oblivious to the fact that she wasn't paying attention. "That other bull was kind of a lightweight, but this one is power on hooves. Mean son of a gun. He's never let a man hear the buzzer, not yet. Those cowboys are crazy to enter. Must be some hot dames for prizes," he said, laughing. "Not to mention a fine heirloom piece—if there's anything left of it."

Nina blinked, her mind racing. Maybe

there was a way to win back her self-respect. "What do you do when your wife's mad at you?" she asked the driver.

"Buy roses. Candy. Write love letters. Anything to get off the couch." He grinned. "Young folks today are only interested in being right. They don't understand the only way to win in marriage is not to care who's right. Me? Sorry's my favorite word. Comes out of my mouth real easy. Kind of like your sister back there. Saying sorry is a bond between friends and family. I *love* saying sorry to my wife. Making up is my *favorite* thing to do."

"What does she do when you're mad at her?"

"Now, there's the key to a good marriage," the driver said. "I don't get mad at her. It's a waste of time and a circular maze. The lady is *always* right, even if she's wrong. Now that may sound to some folks like I lack self-respect, but you see, I'd rather sleep in my bed next to my soft woman and be wrong than sleep on the sofa with a spineful of springs and righteousness."

Nina smiled and leaned back against the seat. "Take me to the rodeo, please, sir."

"What about your plane?"

She looked out the window. "There'll be another plane tomorrow, and a fifty-dollar transfer fee is a small price to pay to get back what is mine."

"Yes, ma'am," the driver said, grinning at her in the rearview mirror. "The lady is *always* right."

Chapter Ten

Navarro waited anxiously for the event to be called. The bed was in the middle of the arena, the subject of the packed crowd's great interest. Instead of the pretty white linens Nina used on the bed, a red satin bedspread graced the mattress and red-satin pillowcases covered the pillows. A few lace-edged, heart-shaped throw pillows were scattered on top and pinwheels had been placed along the headboard and footboard. Air from the old wall fans turned the pinwheels, guaranteeing that if the cowboys didn't make Bloodthirsty take notice, the pinwheels would be sure to grab his attention.

Marvella had overbooked the event. Generally four cowboys "played cards" at the table, each trying to be the last one seated. There were ten cowboys participating in this event. Navarro figured that was due to the take Delilah had gotten out of her sister for charity, but it didn't matter. He was ready to rock. Flexing his fingers, Navarro smiled, thinking about his little librarian safe and sound under Crockett's auspices. It was nice to have a twin to help when things got rough. They'd started out watching Nina together, and before this day was done, they'd have Nina and her possessions at Malfunction Junction—where they belonged.

"Scoot over, hero," a little cowboy next to him said.

He would have taken offense at the snippy tone except he was in too good of a mood. Moving away from the window, he went to peruse the Jefferson box. Full of family and friends as always, he spotted newly shaven Last, Archer, Bandera, Calhoun and Delilah and Jerry. Most of the Union Junction stylists were there, as well as several of the girls from Delilah's salon.

It was great to be a hero in front of the hometown crowd. They'd watched many a Jefferson brother test his mettle on this sawdust floor—always good to walk away, winner or loser, knowing there was family waiting to applaud his efforts.

He loved being a Malfunction Junction cowboy.

"Which makes it double unfortunate that I fell for a gal who has no intent to settle south of Kentucky," he muttered, squaring his hat on his head.

However, Nina was at the ranch, safe and sound, where she belonged—for the moment—so he could focus on the business at hand. He walked over to join the other cowboys hanging alongside the rail, checking out the competition.

"Heard Bloodthirsty knows he's getting cowboy stew for dinner," one said. "Said he passed on lunch so he'd get his full share of a meal."

"I heard it was more like cowboy margarita, shaken and stirred," another said.

One cracked his knuckles.

The shortest cowboy—who'd called him hero—merely remained at the rail, staring out at the bed. Obviously new to rodeo, since he didn't talk to anyone and was wearing new jeans. He even had his hat facing the wrong way. Navarro thought he spied a price tag poking up from the side of the jeans.

Dimestore cowboy—poor devil probably thinks rodeo is child's play. Bang, bang, shoot-'em-up, walk away rich.

Navarro put his boot on the rail next to the other cowboy and braced his forearms over the wood. "Nervous?"

"No." The little cowboy walked away.

"Hmm." Navarro glanced at the man standing next to him, who'd seen the huffy cowboy walk away from Navarro's friendly overture.

"Short man syndrome," the blue-shirted, older cowboy said kindly. "Rather Napoleonic of him."

"Yeah," Navarro agreed. "It's always the little ones who have all the attitude."

They laughed congenially for a minute, then reached over to shake hands. "May the best man win," the man said.

"The best man," agreed Navarro. Still, he glanced after the short cowboy, who'd found himself a corn dog to eat.

"Whew, wouldn't eat that before an event." Still, he admired the cowboy's grit. Amazed, he watched the small cowboy polish off a large paper cup of tea and then a plastic bowl of fruit. "Maybe he'll grow," he said to his companion.

"Probably he'll bow out when he sees Bloodthirsty coming at him," the man said. "And I don't envy the cowboy standing next to him when he blows."

Navarro laughed. "Good point. I'll be sure to stay away."

He heard the announcer call the event. "Gotta go, man," Navarro said. "Let's cowboy up."

"I'm only in it for the glory," his companion said. "I call the backside of the bed, 'cause I ain't hanging around long."

Navarro had figured his new friend might be a bit old for such a daredevil sport. "What's the point, then?"

The man grinned. "Lady friend thinks the bed is beautiful. Says she'll marry me if I win it. Ain't gonna win it, but figure I'll get points for trying. I sure would like to get my girl to the altar."

"Ouch." *Maybe I should have thought to drag that promise out of Nina.*

The announcer began introducing the

event and the cowboys filed toward the bed, each staking a claim where they thought they might be able to perch the longest. The little, food-stuffing cowboy ambled out last, just as Navarro settled into his spot.

Navarro chuckled to himself. "Short man syndrome," he muttered, and the little cowboy turned to stare at him defiantly for just a second from his spot front-and-center on the bed. Just like a novice. Any greenhorn should know the worst spot to be was closest to the bull and dead in its sight.

"Angry little cow-elf," the friendly cowboy whispered to Navarro. "Probably last on the stack, if you know what I mean."

Navarro nodded, uneasily looking over to Bloodthirsty's chute. The cowboys were struggling with loading the bull. There was bucking and kicking going on. Someone yelled and suddenly the gate burst open.

Navarro's blood seemed to curdle as his eyes focused on the bull. Never had he seen anything that bent on destruction running straight for him. It was as if Marvella had whispered in its ear, "Get my money's worth out of those cowboys," and the bull was obeying, to the crowd's delight. Images of Roman coliseums ran through his mind as the people cheered the bull, and suddenly, the friendly cowboy next to him said, "I'm outta here." He escaped, jumping up on the rail before the bull ever made it to the middle of the arena.

Navarro tensed, knowing he had two more seconds before the bull rushed the bed. The little cowboy stood, waving his thin arms at the bull.

For a small man, he had a great ass. Kinda round and—

"Get down!" he yelled at the greenhorn, jerking him down by the back of his shirt. The two of them tumbled to the center of the bed for just an instant—long enough for the little cowboy's hat to fall off, revealing blond, bunned hair, a dirt-smeared cheek and eyes he couldn't forget if he wanted to.

"Nina," he breathed. "You little witch."

She shrugged away from him so she could get back to the front of the bed. Navarro felt the first rush of air as Bloodthirsty went by, following a fleeing cowboy. Navarro grasped for Nina's shirt collar again, but she flung her arm back. He caught her, giving her a good jerk, but she fell back into the bed.

"If you don't get the H. A. Rey outta here, I'm gonna be awful mad when this is over," he shouted. "Go on!"

With all her might, Nina shoved Navarro back onto the bed. The last two remaining cowboys moved to the rail, realizing Bloodthirsty was heading their way, hooves and horns flying.

"Why is Navarro fighting with that little cowboy?" Archer asked, munching popcorn. "It's not sporting to pick on such a little 'un. Plus, you're not supposed to thrash your opponent so you can win the event."

"Is he fighting, or is there something we should know about him?" Bandera asked, peering down. "Seems they know each other pretty well."

"Huh," Calhoun said. "He musta taken Nina's leavin' harder than we thought he would. Look at him trying to drag that little thing into the middle of the bed with him. If I didn't know my brother better, I'd think he'd lost his mind."

"That's not a little cowboy," Last said. "That's a little fake cowgirl." He sat down, dumbfounded. "No wonder Navarro's out there losing his mind! It's the Curse of the Broken Body Parts—getting injured means he's *really* in love."

"He's gonna take a blow to the pants if he doesn't look sharp." Bandera jumped to his feet, cupping his hands to his mouth. "Navarro! Look out!"

It was too late. Bloodthirsty hit the bed with a huge whack heard through the arena. Everyone gasped. Flailing, Nina and Navarro fell into the center of the bed, him on top of her, knocking the breath from both of them.

The bed collapsed.

"That curse didn't hurt like I thought it would," Navarro said.

"Damn," Last said, eating Bandera's popcorn as the clowns ran to try to turn Bloodthirsty away from the wreckage on the floor. "*Now* I remember jumping on that bed. It's all coming back to me."

"Stupid-head!" Calhoun said to Last before hurdling the rail to the floor to help Navarro.

"If it wasn't for you, we wouldn't even be here, dunce," Bandera said to Last, following Calhoun.

Archer sighed and headed over the rail after his brothers.

Last put his popcorn down as he watched his brothers.

After the bull pranced once around the ring, snorting and seeming to take his applause from the audience, Bloodthirsty was shooed into the breezeway by the clowns.

Delilah brushed Nina's hair from her face. "Are you hurt, honey?"

"I'm fine, thank you," Nina said, staring at Navarro. "I would have been better if *he* hadn't landed on me."

"I would have been better if *she* had stayed at home where *she* belongs," Navarro replied.

Nina gasped. "You're *crazy*."

"And no librarian worth her Dewey decimals would ever do something this zany. Have you lost your mind?"

"Maybe. Maybe I did. But I've got it

back now," she snapped, putting her hands on her hips.

He gave an exasperated sigh. "I should have seen right through that disguise. There's so much blue in those jeans, your skin is probably dyed. No self-respecting cowboy dresses like that."

"Well, you didn't see through my disguise. I was under your nose the whole time!"

"I thought you were out of harm's way at home!" He tried to ignore the scary pounding in his chest. "I've never seen you eat like you did before the event, either."

Nina gave him a disgusted look. "If we knew each other better, you'd know that I always eat when I'm nervous, which isn't often, because I'm a librarian and my life isn't that exciting," she said. "But we don't know each other that well, so we shouldn't be surprised that I could be on the very same bed with you and you wouldn't know it!"

He grunted, annoyed. "Remember when you told me the story about the hero who left his heroine by the stream with only a shirt, and I said I'd never leave my heroine alone like that?"

"Yes," Nina said. "Only *this* heroine was smart enough not to stay where there was danger, and she got up and walked away *on her own* two feet."

"And *that*," Navarro said, "is why they didn't have a happy ending."

They glared at each other.

"And the winner of the Cowboy Bed Check event, the bed, the dates with the most beautiful women anyplace, and the purse is," Marvella called over the microphone, holding up the trophy, "Nina and Navarro Jefferson!"

They both turned to stare at Marvella.

Navarro looked back at Nina. "Did she just say what I think she said?"

"No. She didn't." Nina waved to some men in the stands, motioning for them to come take the bed. "You can keep the dates. I don't want them. Try going commando on them." She brushed the sawdust off her new jeans.

"What about the money?"

She turned, walking away. "I got what I came for. And now, I'm going *home*."

In the stands, Last watched his brother and Nina stride to opposite ends of the arena, each going their separate way. The movers collected the bed, or the pieces of it. Marvella stood holding the trophy and the check, somewhat confused as to why her big moment had deflated. The audience filed from the arena, with the exception of a few curious children and adults looking at the broken bed being packed away.

Sighing, Last headed out.

"Where ya headed, son?" the friendly blue-shirted cowboy asked him.

"Don't know yet," Last said.

"I'm gonna hit the next rodeo on the circuit. Gonna try to win something else for my girlfriend. She had her heart set on this bed, and I figure I'd best take something home to her. Wanna ride?"

"Why not?" Last said dully. "Maybe my luck will change."

Chapter Eleven

Navarro took about five minutes to rethink his argument where Nina was concerned, then ran after her, catching her outside the arena watching the movers load up her bed. "Wait, Nina," he said. "How are you getting home?"

"Plane," she said curtly.

He didn't let that bother him. "How about truck, instead?"

She turned to stare at him. "What?"

Navarro took a deep breath. "I'm thinking the least I can do is drive you home."

"Why would I want you to do that?" Nina demanded. "I already have a ticket. I'd be home quickly."

Navarro nodded. "Yes, but you should consider the scenic route. We only live once, and I happen to know you have a bit o' the wild in you. Not every woman dresses up like a man to win her bed back."

"It was history," Nina said. "Heritage. It was hope for the future. It's not just a bed that I won."

He nodded. "I know. And this is not just any offer to take you home. This is my effort to help you live out the romance of your fantasies. And in this one people don't *not* see each other for six years, marry other people or get carried off by forest creatures. I told you that a hero would never leave his woman behind. I meant that. It's dangerous."

"I think I'll be safe on a plane."

"Oh, swamp creatures with big nostrils and flat heads like to fly, too. Trust me on this."

"You got very stuck on my made-up novel."

"I got very stuck on the fact that you tested me. Time and time again, you've tested the limits of my patience, my endurance and my sense of humor." He grinned. "I'm ready to pass the final test."

"Which is?"

"Can I make it on Delaware soil with a peachy librarian?"

"Not much of a test," she said. "It's a great place to live."

"But it's not Malfunction Junction."

"And then there's that," she said brightly. "You do make your points shine."

"Actually, I have a theory that a man doesn't really know a woman until he's spent the weekend with her. It's sort of a family caveat. Women are different when you get them out of their comfort zone."

She tried not to smile.

"I saw that," he said. "It's an admission of truth you could not conceal."

"I think it's highly likely that a woman doesn't know a man until they've spent a weekend alone together. A man needs his cave, his wing-backed chair, if you will. Whereas a woman carries most of her cave in her purse." She turned away as the movers closed the truck door.

"Nina," he said. "We're nearly family now. I'd like to elevate our relationship from sexually charged acquaintances to possible holiday dinner companions."

"So," she said, turning to face him,

"you're offering to drive me home, spending three days in a truck with me, without a sexual relationship."

He stood straight as a Boy Scout. "I can do it—if you can."

"What makes you think that would be an attractive offer to me?"

That stopped him. "Because I don't want you to assume I'm only after your body."

"Are you? Would you be, if you could get past your code of gentlemanly honor?"

"Er, actually I have no code like that," he said. "I'm just trying to do anything to spend more time with you. If you want to throw lovemaking into the deal, I can honestly say I will ratify that with enthusiasm."

She laughed.

"On the other hand, if you are not of a mind to share more than scenic routes with me, I will honor that, too. I may go insane, but I wouldn't offer to drive a woman to Delaware just to have sex with her. Heck, I just won a bunch of dates with beautiful women. I guess I could go—"

"You can stop there," Nina said, holding up a hand. "No further clarification needed."

"On second thought," Navarro said, glancing toward the arena. "Since you already have a plane ticket—"

Nina grabbed his sleeve, tugging him toward the truck. "Okay, cowboy, you've dangled the bait long enough. I'm biting. Let's see if we can stand each other for three days closed up in a truck."

"Actually, the tricky part," Navarro said happily, "is what you're going to do with me once you get me to Delaware. I want to work in the library and learn all about the card catalog system."

"Well, that's the first thing we're going to change about you," Nina said. "You obviously haven't been in a library since the computer age began."

"Not to mention," Navarro said, enjoying being dragged to his truck, "I live in a rural town with a small population. We hardly ever update. The computer age completely missed us."

"Right. This from a man whose parents educated him on the classics and Latin."

"That's right, H. A. Rey." Navarro pulled

out his keys. "There's just one thing we've got to agree upon up front. Don't try to fold my map for me."

Nina laughed. "You win the first round."

"This is gonna be easy," Navarro said.

"COULD THIS BE ANY HARDER?" Nina said a few hours later, staring at the engine as it smoked heavily. "I missed my plane for the scenic route, not to be broken down in the Texas panhandle with you."

"It just sets us back a few hours," Navarro said. "I hope."

Nina crossed her legs from her seat on the ground in front of the garage, watching the mechanic diligently work on the truck. "I drive an old Jeep."

He turned to look at her. "Really?"

"Mmm. I feel very preppy in it, and I don't freak like other people when we get snow, and mostly, I like sitting up a little higher than I would in a car."

"Jeeps are good. My truck's pretty new," he said sorrowfully. "I wouldn't have expected this."

"Put molasses in your engine often?" the mechanic asked.

"Hell, no," Navarro said, standing up. "I treat that truck like an expensive whor—I mean, I lavish care and money upon that vehicle."

"Well, somebody ran you a bad joke then," the mechanic said. "Any ideas?"

"None." Navarro glanced at Nina. "I'd suspect you of many things, but since you're with me, I'll guess you're not the culprit. Unless you wanted to be stuck with me longer?"

"No," Nina said, happily dashing his hopeful expression. "Ask me again when the scenery is better." She glanced around the dingy garage.

Navarro sighed. "Do what you gotta do, man. I guess I'd better phone home and tell them I'm taking an extensive weekend to hunt deer."

Nina laughed. "They'll believe you not at all."

"I know. Trolls." Navarro dialed his cell phone and grinned when Crockett hollered, "Malfunction Junction!" into the phone. "Crockett, what's up?"

"Nothing good, bro," his twin said hurriedly. "Nina's missing. She tricked me by sending me off for food. I swear I never saw that coming!"

"Oh, sorry, Crockett. I forget how slow news is to travel. Nina and I won the Bed Check and now we've hit the road for Delaware."

There was silence on the other end of the phone for a moment.

"Delaware?" Crockett finally said. "I guess a man would be hard-pressed not to follow that full-size, bountiful booty just about anywhere. Even north. I reckon even I would have leaped at the opportunity to—"

"Crockett," Navarro said on a growl, "I'm gonna end up spearing you over holiday dinner if you don't find your own peach to pit."

Crockett laughed, then said, "Listen, Navarro. Seriously, man, you gotta come home. Last is gone."

Navarro rubbed his face tiredly, then glanced over at Nina. She was still sitting in front of the garage. She'd pulled off her shoes and was inspecting her toenails. Suddenly, Navarro's bad mood leaked away.

She had very delicate feet.

"One day, I'm going to hold those feet in the palm of my hand," he said. "I may even suck those toes, if I'm lucky."

"What?" Crockett's voice was loud with surprise.

"Never mind. You're going to have to hold down the fort for the weekend, dude. And don't feel bad about Nina giving you the slip. She's in a break-out period, and I, for one, am enjoying capitalizing on her new-found sense of adventure. The stress may kill me, but I'm determined not to leave this planet without enjoying her particular ride."

"Man, you have got it so bad," Crockett said. "I almost envy you the fever. Almost, but not quite. I nearly crapped an egg when I found Nina had outwitted me. And I'm not through talking to Valentine about her compliance in the plot."

Navarro laughed. "Sisters." He watched with great interest as Nina dug some polish out of her purse to paint her toenails pink.

"'Bye," Navarro said, no longer paying attention to Crockett. He strode over to Nina, watching her glide the pretty rose color on her toes. "Marry me," he said.

"What?" She glanced up at him, startled, her mouth half open with a surprised giggle that died when she saw the look in his eyes. "Are you…all right?"

"I don't know that I'll ever be right now that I've had you. I think you're permanently embedded in my bloodstream."

Nina smiled. "You're a wild man. I'll overlook the spur-of-the-moment proposal since you just got off the phone with your family. They always seem to make you a little edgy."

He groaned and sat beside her. "Did the mechanic say how long it would take to order an engine for the truck?"

"He said he had a brother who was driving one over from the nearest city. It shouldn't be bad. Only a couple of hours."

She smiled at him, and he could feel the furrows between his eyebrows melt away.

"How's the ranch?"

"Malfunctioning as always," Navarro said crossly. "Crockett claims Last is gone, but you know what that means."

"Tell me."

He shrugged. "Liquor store. Tattoo parlor. Piercing palace."

"Why would he do that?"

"I don't know. I thought he'd straightened up for a little bit." Navarro scratched his head and tried to focus on Nina's paint job. "Maybe he's just out visiting the Union Junction salon girls. We do that sometimes because they understand us."

"And it would have nothing to do with having a salon full of females fawning over you," Nina said dryly.

"Not quite your average harem, but closest thing to it," Navarro replied, tweaking her nose. "Don't be jealous, sweetie. I'm not leaving your side."

She ignored that. "Who do you think put molasses in your engine?"

"Well, I would suspect Marvella, but frankly, I think she likes roping the Jefferson brothers into her events too much to cause me such distress. I would have suspected you, but you're here with me, and obviously—"

Nina gasped and dug him with her elbow.

"Okay, okay, so you don't even know where the engine cap is. It wasn't you," he teased, enjoying her outraged expression. "So that leaves a fellow competitor or perhaps a random bad trick by one of the passers-through. It could have been coincidence that my truck was chosen."

Nina put away the polish. "Does seem a bit odd that someone would be carrying molasses around to do harm with."

"Yeah." Navarro broke his constant perusal of Nina's feet and looked around the garage yard. "Of course, they could have stolen some from Marvella, I guess. Maybe it was one of the salon girls...."

Nina straightened. "Navarro."

"Yes, my pet?"

"Remember that stuff Last drank the night he got my sister pregnant? Crockett told me that Fannin's sexually disinterested bull got into the stuff, and after he drank it, he about jumped sky-high with bull... bull-i-ness." She blushed.

Navarro grinned at her. "You sly little kitten," he said. "Do you want me to have some of Marvella's secret soda airfreighted to Delaware for us to sip through straws as we peruse the dusty shelves of ye olde tomes and periodicals?"

"No," Nina said. "Rewind to the other

night. Remember? Crockett drank one or two of those things and went down like a ton of bricks. He said he'd been tired, but what if he'd gotten into a particularly potent batch of brew?"

Navarro tried not to think about sex with Nina, but it was hard not to now that she'd brought the topic up. "Uh, it'll teach him to read the label of the beer he's grabbing?"

"Navarro," Nina said, tugging on his collar to get him to listen. "Heat and sugar make a syrupy mess. Much like molasses."

"Aha," he said. "I follow. You think one of the Cut-n-Gurls hit my engine with Marvella's sex sauce."

"Actually, what I think," Nina said slowly, realizing that the three-day trip was about to become quite long because of the words she was about to say, "is that Last's recent bouts of drunkenness weren't caused by beer, they were caused by Marvella's wild-making brew. It doesn't take a genius to suspect your brother of this mess."

Chapter Twelve

"Why would Last do that?" Navarro asked, dumbfounded.

"Why would he dye his hair? Pierce his ear? Channel David Bowie?" Nina asked, exasperated.

"Nina, you don't understand. He's always been the family compass, the rock in the storm that stayed strong and unyielding." Navarro shook his head. "Last's hit a rough patch, but he's just having trouble with this pregnancy thing."

"'This pregnancy thing,'" Nina said, "happens to involve my sister. And it's a baby, by the way, not a thing."

"I know. I know." Navarro frowned. "But Last wouldn't do anything to the truck. A man's livelihood rests on his wheels. We respect our trucks. We worship them. A man's truck is his—"

"Navarro," Nina said. "Did Last tell you that he and Valentine took a walk together the other night?"

"No. But he takes many walks he doesn't register with me."

"Can I borrow your phone?"

"Sure." Navarro handed it to her. "What's up?"

"I want to talk to Valentine. Will you dial your house, the one we're staying in?"

He looked at the phone for a moment. "I don't think I know the phone number. Hang on a second."

"How can you not know your phone number?"

"Because I don't call myself. Shh," Navarro said, punching some numbers into the cell phone. "Hello? Valentine? How are you doing? Good, good. Feeling all right?" He listened for a moment. "Excellent. When you see my twin, will you have him send a care package to Nina's house? I can buy a toothbrush, some toothpaste, all that garb, and I have a change of clothes in the trunk, but I might need one more days' worth of duds." He listened again. "Yes, she's behaving herself. Here, you can talk to her."

"Valentine," Nina said, once on the phone, "when you and Last talked the other night, how did it go? Tell me again, don't leave out any details."

"Fine," Valentine said. "We both agreed we didn't know each other well enough to share more than parenting duties. And we agreed to talk again next week. Slowly iron matters out between us."

"Anything get said that you thought was out of the ordinary?"

"No, not really," Valentine said. "You know how these boys are. They run their mouths constantly."

"And when he was running his, did he seem happy about everything?"

"Well, of course, he thinks his brothers ride him too hard. He says they expect too much. Because he's the baby, they can sometimes be harsh."

"I thought the baby of the family was raised on benign neglect or over-spoiling."

"We've definitely done all of that," Navarro murmured, blowing out a breath. He picked up her hand. Across the yard, the mechanic was checking the fluids under the hood of his truck.

"So," Valentine continued, "I don't know what all the dynamics of our new family are, but as far as Last and myself, we've decided to wait and see. There's never going to be any 'us,' but we will be parents. And I won't say this decision doesn't hurt, but I think it hurts him just as much, in a different way."

"He seems to have lots of problems," Nina said. "I wouldn't recommend him for you, to be honest."

"Hey!" Navarro said. "That's my brother."

"I'll call you later, sweetie," she said to Valentine. "I'm taking the long road home with Navarro, and we've encountered a ruined engine, so it's guaranteed to be a long trip."

"I heard you got the bed back, though."

"In pieces." Nina rolled her eyes. "Everything's broken. Rest as much as possible, Valentine. I'll call you soon." She hung up.

"I'll help you fix your bed again, after

my engine's replaced," Navarro said. "You know I can do it."

"Yes," Nina said, "I know you can fix beds."

"Hey, when that bull hit the bed, were you scared?"

Nina looked at him. "I was scared the whole time."

"I should spank you for that stunt. Do you know, when I realized it was you wearing that silly get-up, you completely shot my concentration?"

Nina laughed. "You don't have any concentration that I've ever noticed."

"Yeah, well. That's because I started losing it when you came around. 'Fix my bed,'" he mimicked. "Before I knew it, I wanted to test it for myself. Hey," he said, sitting up, "when do I get a run in the charmed heirloom bed? I want to see if it works!"

"It works. Valentine and Last proved it."

"Yeah, but *we* like each other. In fact we like each other so much, we'd probably fire up triplets!"

"No turn for you, Navarro. Because

when I test the charm, it's going to be the *old-fashioned* way."

"I did propose."

"In jest," Nina said, "and I actually count that against you. You faker. I'm sure the charm frowns upon fakers. In fact, it would probably backfire because of your lack of sincerity."

Navarro stood to pace. "I don't envision Last sabotaging my truck," he said, changing the subject yet again.

"I know."

"I mean, that'd be like me saying Valentine got pregnant on purpose because she's spoiled and she's the youngest and had a temper tantrum."

Nina stiffened. "Navarro, your illustration is poor."

"But you know it's true."

"I don't want to talk about it anymore." Nina got up and walked away.

"But we have to." He caught up to her. "The basic underlying theme here is lack of responsibility. Valentine and Last aren't right for each other because each of them are the youngest, and each has lived with siblings bailing them out and rescuing them. Neither of them has ever had to face the harsh light of their actions. I'll admit Last has done some real dumb things lately, but Valentine—"

"Valentine what?" Nina demanded. "Just wanted to trap a husband? Just remember, you proposed to *me,* Navarro." She stared up at him, suddenly angry that this cowboy could think the things he did about her family. "You may have proposed to me in jest, but I said no for real. And believe me, I wouldn't have you if you were the last male on earth."

Four hours later, after the engine was repaired and they were on the road, Navarro realized he'd stuck his boot in it bigtime. Nina wasn't having anything to do with him; in fact, she alternated between snoozing and listening to music through earphones.

And, blast her, she did it all in the back seat of the crew-cab truck.

This was not how he'd envisioned his scenic trip to Delaware. Oh, the scenery outside was pretty, but the scenery he'd meant to take in was Nina.

Hard to enjoy a lady's company when she'd set up residence behind him. Cramming a small powdery doughnut into his mouth from the package he'd bought at the gas station, Navarro tried to think of a way to break the silence. "Want one?" He raised his hand to dangle a tiny doughnut over his shoulder.

The doughnut was lifted from his fingers. He sighed and stopped the truck. "Okay, out," he said to Nina. "We talk now."

She looked at him, her eyes big and accusing, but she didn't move.

"I shouldn't have said it, Nina. I'm sorry."

"It's what you're thinking about my sister. I don't appreciate you assuming she's trying to take advantage of your family. She may be a bit weak-willed, but she's going to get a job, and she's not planning on mooching off you forever. I gave her the purse I won—"

"We won."

"Not exactly." She glared at him. "I won it, because you shouldn't have been there in the first place."

He watched her eat the doughnut, licking the powder off her lips with a little pink tongue. He wanted to kiss her, but his ego receptors were indicating now might not be a good time. She was still tense with him. "Why, Nina? Why are you so much the opposite of your sister? There's no in-between with you two. One of you is hard-headed and independent, and the other is soft and dependent." He waved his hands once, frustrated. "Did it ever occur to you that I might enjoy taking care of you once in a while?"

"You're taking me home. That's quite enough."

He leaned into the truck and hauled her gently out. "Out of your shell, Nina. I'm not taking care of you—you already had a plane ticket. All I did was think of a way to prolong being with you. It's just not working very well."

She sniffed. "You insulted my family's integrity."

"And you suggested Last poured something drastic into my engine."

"I can't apologize, Navarro," she said sadly, "because I think your brother has a problem. I mean, we all have problems and make mistakes, but he's angry with all of you and you don't want to see it."

"He wouldn't destroy my truck."

Nina shook her head. "I didn't want to have to say this, and it's really none of my business, but—"

He stared at her. "What?"

"Did you ever wonder how I came by this guess? It's not like I have a behavioral science degree or anything."

"No. Women just like to opine," Navarro said, aware he wasn't winning any points but needing to say how he felt. "Men don't jump to conclusions as easily. Our feet are pretty stuck to the ground."

"Maybe so stuck that you don't ever get off a bad base." Nina took a deep breath. "Navarro, when I went outside to oversee the movers loading my bed, I saw your brother with his head underneath the hood of your truck."

Her eyes sparkled with sadness, but still he stood motionless with disbelief. "There's an explanation. Nina, Last is my brother. He wouldn't sabotage me. We all work too hard at the ranch."

"I don't think he's himself, Navarro," Nina said carefully. "I think something's pushed him past his breaking point. Maybe it was Marvella's brew. Maybe it was getting Valentine pregnant. I don't know. But the fact is, you shouldn't be here with me."

They looked at each other for a long moment, then she touched his lips. "Navarro, I'm sorry. There can be nothing but lust between you and me."

He couldn't bear the pain inside him. In all his life, he'd never experienced anything like it. "Ever?"

"I don't know. What I do know is that it's not going to happen until you find your brother. Family doesn't turn its back on its own in times of trouble. You should be looking for him, instead of wasting time with me."

Wasting time with her. Time was not wasted with Nina. He adored her.

But she was right in one way he could not overlook: Last was in trouble.

He couldn't ignore the truth any longer. "You may be right."

"It's not a matter of right or wrong," Nina said, thinking about the taxi driver's words. "It's a matter of an unborn baby who will need to know his father one day. A whole father, who knows his family cares enough to find him and draw him back into the circle."

"You're wonderful," he told Nina. "You make me insane, but every part of me craves you, and right now, if you weren't so right, I'd make love to you in my truck and thank you in every way my body possibly knows how for being so smart and caring."

"Eek." Nina glanced up and down the highway. "Don't tempt me, cowboy. I've explored the lusty librarian fantasy. I could go skank any second. Let's not push our luck."

"Come with me," he said.

She laughed. "Be irresponsible and quit my job?"

"Yes. I'll make it worth your while."

"You're crazy. I can't do that!" She shook her head at him. "Navarro, a woman does not give up employment for a man. Not even a sexy-to-the-bone cowboy."

"I need you."

The pull was strong, but she knew she

had to resist. Probably she had known that the instant the bed had collapsed on them in the arena. Navarro only thought he was crazy about her because she was his living fantasy. But she was no fantasy girl. She was plain-Jane vanilla, a librarian by vocation and avocation. "You need no one."

He gently framed her face with his palms. "I," he said, kissing her right cheek. "Need," he said, kissing her left cheek. "You." His lips found hers, not as gently as they'd been on her cheeks, more demanding and insistent than she was expecting. Her blood instantly answered the call as she crazily kissed him back.

"Nina," he whispered against her lips, "if I were a sultan, I'd carry you away on my horse. If I were a wealthy playboy, I'd sweep you out to sea on my yacht. I'd take you by storm and by force and make you mine until the only name you ever remembered was Navarro. But," he said, sliding his hands into her back pockets to tug her against his groin, "I'm just a cowboy. I want to make love to you as many times as I can, every chance I get. I want you with me so that you're never out of my sight, and so that I can have you whenever I want you. That's what I'm talking about."

The kisses he rained along her collarbone and down to where her shirt parted above her breasts spoke hotly of his desire for her, and Nina thought she was going to sink right down onto the hot, dusty pavement.

But he pulled away, still holding her face, staring down into her eyes. The passion she saw in his gaze took her breath away.

"Say yes," he said. "Say you want to be with me."

It was madness, insanity. A librarian didn't go trolling around in a truck in the countryside with a man whose one stated goal was to love her senseless.

"Yes," she said, surprising even herself. "You've got yourself a shotgun rider. For better or worse, I'm moving my things to the front seat."

"Now the good times begin," Navarro said. "It's me and you and the pretzel bag on the good ol' southern highways of Texas. All I need now is a dog in the truck bed. Maybe a cooler in the back. And feel free to read me your romance novel while I drive. I'll be the happiest man on the planet. Crockett won't ever read to me, and he almost always insists I drive."

"This is probably not going to be pretty," Nina said, trying to ignore him by brushing doughnut powder off the seat. "Traveling companions should have common interests."

"We do," Navarro said. "And we're going to find them while we look for Last."

She glanced up. "Not sexual interests. *Real* common interests."

Navarro grinned, confident in his masculinity. "Nina, the mention of sex was what got you to say yes. Let's not tinker with what works, all right?"

Chapter Thirteen

Nina nodded. "Very typical of a man to disguise his emotions under the verb of sex." She took her seat, primly crossing her legs at the ankles.

Navarro started the truck. "Nina, sex is not a verb."

"It is when you talk about it."

Rubbing his chin, he said, "I never thought about it that way, but you could be right."

"Shall I read?" Nina asked, pulling out the novel he'd mentioned.

"Not yet. Let me hear you define me some more. It's so interesting."

Nina laughed. "Navarro, you are so needy."

"I believe I did admit that of my own free will. I said, 'Nina, I need you.'"

She looked at him, serious now. "There are times when I wonder how much of what you say is horse puckey."

"Oh, horse puckey is good for growing roses, but not much else." He grinned at her before turning back to the road.

"What will you say to Last when you find him?" Nina asked. "I'm really worried about him."

"Why? He's not your problem."

"He is. We're all part of one big happy family now."

"Well," Navarro said, "I think I'll wait to see what he says to me before I open my mouth."

"Good plan."

"Gotta have one," Navarro agreed. "Although I do find that plans don't work very well with you."

Nina snapped her fingers. "You know why? Because we're missing a connection."

"Hmm, not sure I know what one is."

"Most married couples don't know how to make them. It's an art of conscious desire."

"Are we getting married?" Navarro

asked. "I don't have my tux with me. And I'm already conscious of my desire, thank you, painfully so."

"Here's how we make a connection. You tell me your favorite food and I'll tell you mine."

"That's easy. Pork chops."

"Ew." Nina blinked. "I don't eat any pork at all."

"Did we just miss our connection?"

Nina nodded. "Maybe that was too hard. Let's try something more basic. What's your favorite color?"

"Black."

"No." Nina stared at him. "It is not."

"Ask anybody. Why would I lie, anyway?"

Navarro's tone was so injured that Nina sighed. "Black is the absence of all color."

"It's still my favorite. Yours?"

"Green. Any shade. Although I do get very happy when I see deep forest greens. That piney effect feels very homey to me."

"There's hardly any piney effects where we live," Navarro said. "It's all dry and yellow and sandy."

"I know," Nina said. "Hard to miss that fact."

"Let me try a connection. What's your favorite kind of music?"

Nina thought for a moment. "I like everything, but I prefer classical piano."

"I thought you might say the Captain and Tennille-type happy music."

"No," Nina said, "but I bought their record once."

"I like jazz, especially with a great sax." Navarro grinned. "Bet you thought I'd say country music."

"No," Nina said. "I didn't think you'd be obvious."

They sat silently for a moment.

"You know," Nina said, "I think Last felt that he'd let you down."

"By messing up my truck?"

"By bringing a woman into the family you all had no connection with. Valentine and I will never be anything like any of you. We're just too different from you guys."

"I believe differences are good, to a point." Navarro waved at a passing state trooper. "However, similarities sure can make life easy. None of my brothers married women who were similar to them, but they all had that deep-down core of something that made them love each other."

"A connection."

"I guess," Navarro said. "Could you ever love me?"

Nina hesitated. "I suppose I think it would be impossible for me to let myself feel that."

"Love isn't something you allow. It just happens. I think it's happening for me and not you," he said.

"Navarro." Nina looked at him with surprise. "You don't love me."

"I didn't say I did," Navarro said, "I said I think. *Think* is just as important a verb as *sex*."

Nina blinked. "To whom? Academics? Writers?"

"To a man," Navarro stressed. "We understand the importance of thinking about sex."

"Sex is a noun in that sentence," Nina pointed out. "Or to be more technical, it's an object of the prepositional phrase. Wait, were we using a noun or a verb the other night in your bed?"

"We were smart," Navarro said. "We were using a condom."

"Oh, gosh." Nina laid her head back against the headrest. "I'm going to take a nap."

"Good. Put your bare tootsies up on the seat and let me hold them."

Nina's body stiffened. "I am not going to do that."

"Why? You'll like me massaging your feet."

She moved her feet farther away from him nervously. "I just can't."

"I'd do it for you. If you wanted to massage me."

"Yes, but I'd rather you didn't." Nina tried not to laugh. "In fact, I'm not sure why I'd ever want to massage a man's foot."

"To make him happy." Navarro tugged on her hair lightly. "Do you know how many pleasure receptors are in the human foot?"

"Navarro," Nina said sternly, deciding a nap wasn't wise. "Let's focus on your brother." She dug the map out of the glove box, unfolding it to gauge the distance they had to travel. "Where are you heading first?"

"If he's not at home, and the brothers have checked all the usual spots, and he's not in Lonely Hearts Station—which he's not if he really did damage my truck on purpose, then I'm guessing we start at the next rodeo on the circuit."

"Why?"

"Because your sister said he'd mentioned getting away. They talked about how they both wished their lives hadn't been turned upside down by the baby. Connection, you know."

"Yes, although not one to build a relationship on."

"No." Navarro pointed to a spot on the map. "That's where we're headed."

"I've never heard of that town," Nina said.

"Most people haven't, especially Dannonians. That's why you're going to enjoy a long truck ride through Texas. There's more to these dusty yellow plains than you could ever imagine. Fold the map nicely, please, or don't fold it at all."

"I'm so excited," Nina said, trying not to annoy Navarro's peculiar gene by folding his map on the wrong creases. "After we find him, I'm going back home."

"I know," Navarro said. "And you'll have plenty of stories to tell your friends about all the wild fun you enjoyed here in Texas." He glanced at her. "You never mention your girlfriends. Or boyfriends. How come you don't talk much about your life in Dannon?"

"Because you're always talking." Nina laid her head against the window and closed her eyes. "Turn on that sax jazz you were talking about," she said. "All this craziness has made me tired."

"Sexual attraction will do that to you," Navarro said. "Just wear you out until you finally give in to it."

Nina laughed. "I'll be fine, cowboy. Just drive, okay? Let's find your brother, because I've got to get home someday."

Navarro glanced over at Nina as she closed her eyes, a slight smile on her face as she got comfortable.

Not if I have anything to do with it, he thought. *You're a keeper.*

THEY FOUND LAST in Golden, Texas, hanging around the chutes, watching cowboys watch each other. He didn't seem to be interacting with anybody, and suddenly, Navarro was struck by an uneasy realization that Nina was right: Last needed him.

"Bro," he said, going to stand beside him while Nina hung back at the concession booth. She'd already said she didn't think she should be part of their reunion, and now he appreciated her sensitivity. "What are you doing here, man?"

Last shook his head sadly. "Just wandering around. What are you doing here?"

"Looking for you. Why didn't you let someone know where you were going?"

"I didn't know where I was going. I just needed to be gone." Last's face was a picture of misery. "The family's let me know clearly how much I've let them down. I can't take it anymore. I know I messed up. But it's real hard living with the daily reminder of how much I've sunk in everybody's opinion."

Navarro nodded. "I bet it is. But you can't roam around forever. Eventually, you gotta go back home."

Last shrugged. "Seems to be a pattern in our house. Anybody heard from Mason?"

"I don't know."

"It's time for him to get back and face his mess, too. I'm not the only brother that left, Navarro. You left. Everybody's left."

It was true. Now that he thought about it, if they didn't start pulling together as a family, they were going to have to hire outside help with the ranch, which they'd always agreed wasn't the best solution for Malfunction Junction. They had their own ways of doing things—and those ways had always worked.

"Let me drive you home," Navarro said. "That'll at least get one brother back where he belongs. And I'll pound the boys while I'm at it, and tell them to shut their yaps where you're concerned."

Last nodded. "Deal. I've had a bellyful of it. It's not like I know what I'm doing with this baby stuff. Valentine gets lots of support and attention because she's having the baby, but I get the black looks and the disgust. It's scary enough to be a father without everybody gunning for me."

"All right," Navarro said quietly. "I'll have a chat with the boys. You've been punished enough."

"Thanks."

"Last."

"What?" His brother looked at him uneasily.

"Did you put something in my truck engine?"

Last recoiled. "Hell, no. Why would I?"

"I don't know." Navarro stared at him, thinking. "Did you look under my truck hood for something before you left town?"

"Yeah. But only because I saw some people hanging around it. I shooed them away from your truck and then checked under the hood."

"General bystanders looking at a truck in excellent condition," Navarro mused. "What do you know about Marvella's secret sauce?"

Last shook his hands at him. "Never to touch it again. Ever. That stuff is firewater. Don't do it," he said, "if you're thinking about it. It's not worth the trip."

"Whatever she's bottling, it's strong enough to kill a truck engine." Navarro glanced at Nina one last time, his gaze thoughtful. "Who would do that?"

"Who knows?" Last asked. "You may never know the answer. So many people were in town for the rodeo that it could have been anyone who thought it was funny to get their kicks that way. Wait a minute," Last said slowly. "Did she say I did it? Is that why you're here?"

"Nina suggested you needed help," Navarro said smoothly, in the interest of future family relations. "She said you'd seemed sad. And that she was afraid it had to do with her sister."

"Yeah, well." Last relaxed a little. "I wish it hadn't happened, but Valentine's pretty cool. We're going to work things out somehow."

"Good. Come home now."

"All right." Last waved goodbye to someone in the stands, then followed his brother out.

"Who was that?" Navarro asked.

"Some friendly cowboy whose been trying to win something for his girlfriend so she'll marry him. I wouldn't have a woman I felt I had to impress all the time."

Navarro watched Nina walk toward the truck in front of them, her fanny swaying just the way he liked it. "I could watch that woman all day. She impresses me constantly."

Last laughed. "Have you ever considered dating around to get her out of your bloodstream?"

"No," Navarro said definitively. "I'd be bored. Be nice to her. She's the reason we came to get you. She could be home among her books and periodicals by now."

"No, she couldn't," Last said with a grin. "You won't let her go."

"It's a struggle," Navarro admitted. "And I think she's not ready to settle down."

"Who is?" Last sighed. "It should be settle *up*. Then everybody might think hitching is a positive thing. Who wants to settle *down*? Doesn't that have kind of a depressing ring to it? What we're really doing is settling for the future, anyway. It's all so stupid."

Navarro got into the truck. Last got in the back. Nina wore her headphones and read her romance novel, ignoring them both for the moment.

"Wanna settle up?" Navarro asked her.

She held one earphone away from her ear. "What?"

"Nothing," Navarro said. "Nothing at all."

Last laughed. "Pathetic. Don't buy the ring just yet."

"THAT WAS FAST," Valentine said when they pulled up to the house.

"They're pretty predictable men, actually," Nina said, "once you get to know them." She waved to the brothers and went inside with her sister.

"Well, I'm glad you're back." Valentine hugged her. "It's lonely without you. Although I did find a job."

"That's great. Where?"

"At the bakery. Mmm. I'm going to love working there," Valentine said, her eyes sparkling.

"Why are you so happy?" Nina asked. "You're glowing."

"I'm having a baby. I live at a wonderful ranch. I have a new family and a job

I'm going to love. What's wrong with my world?"

"True." Nina tossed her things onto the bed. "One thing about riding around with Navarro is you learn to appreciate the comforts of home. Look at how beautiful this bed is."

"Nina," Valentine said with a laugh, "you might as well just give up and stay here forever."

"No," Nina said. "Never. I'm not as brave as you are. I miss my library. I miss my apartment."

"You'd miss all that," Valentine said, taking her hand, "but you'd have a man."

"A man?" Nina looked at her sister. "That sounds so archaic."

Valentine winked. "You just have one too many feminist genes. Set one of those little genes free and give Navarro a break."

"We have no connection," Nina said. "We have nothing in common."

Her sister laughed. "He'd make a great husband. And he's clearly mad for you. Just as you're wild for him. All this pride stuff just gets in the way, Nina. You should eat some humble pie and win yourself a cowboy with a heart of gold."

"It's not that easy," Nina said. "I hate that get-yourself-a-man thing. Men are not free-range chickens to be caught and tamed."

"Believe it or not, that's exactly what Navarro wants," Valentine said. "You have the fun part. I've got the brother who wants nothing to do with me. Oh, we're fine. We're going to raise a baby together, but that's all we're ever going to have. I know that because Last doesn't look at me the way Navarro looks at you."

"How?"

"Like *you're* the free-range chicken and he hasn't quite figured out how to get you in the box. Nina, when you walked up the porch a minute ago, he didn't take his eyes off you. Last was waving to the air, but Navarro's focus was all on you." Valentine smiled. "It's so sweet."

"It would never last." Which was not the happiest thought in the world. "I'm cautious by nature, you know, and my caution bells are ringing like mad."

"I know. I figured. So, now what?"

"Now that I have everybody where they belong," Nina said, "I'm going home. And do me a favor, okay? This time don't rat me out to Navarro. One thing I have learned—he's not going to let me go." She looked at her sister. "And to be honest, Valentine, I *really* need to get away from him. His intense focus is starting to make me forget I have a life that doesn't include Malfunction Junction."

Valentine looked at her sadly. "Come on. I'll drive you to the airport. Crockett gave me keys so I wouldn't feel penned. He said a woman ought to be able to hit the grocery and the hairdresser when she needed to. You didn't even notice I finally got my hair cut."

"You look fabulous. When I came down here to rescue you, I'll admit I was worried. But now I see you're going to make it just fine."

"Yes, I am," Valentine said. "Thanks for noticing. Can I make one tiny suggestion, from little sister to big sister?"

"Of course." Nina pulled her hair up into a ponytail.

"Tell Navarro goodbye. If you don't, he's

going to come after you. State why you need to leave him."

Nina considered that. "He does say that it's my ways that are foreplay for him. He says I challenge him." She put the brush down on the dresser. "You're right. If I tell him I am returning home, without him, so I can get back to my life, he will understand that I'm saying goodbye."

"Exactly," Valentine said. "And then he won't feel compelled to drag you back."

"I hate to hurt his feelings."

"He'll survive," Valentine said cheerfully. "These men have boatloads of women waiting to embark."

Nina wasn't sure that made her feel better. "All right. I'll do it in the morning."

"But you have to admit you like him," Valentine said. "That much anyone can see."

"I like him," Nina agreed. "In fact, I'm in love with Navarro. That's the major reason I'm determined to leave. Somewhere between his pursuit of me, his kindness to you and his devotion to his family, I fell head over heels in love. But it will never last, not even with the help of our charmed heirloom bed."

Chapter Fourteen

In the middle of the night, Nina awakened, realizing she wasn't sleeping very well. She dreaded having to say goodbye to Navarro, and the thought preyed on her mind. There was no scenario she could imagine where he would just stick out his hand and say, "Happy trails. Been nice knowing you."

For two people who had no common connections they'd spent a lot of time together. Truthfully, her heart was going to be broken. How did you say goodbye to a man who was far from perfect but yet tried so hard to please?

It was no different from the taxi driver putting his wife first, just for the pleasure of always being with her. He'd made a lot of sense.

Unfortunately, Nina couldn't see long-term happiness in their picture. They were from two different worlds, with two different sets of needs. Sighing, she forced her eyes shut.

Until the window slid up. Gasping, she sat straight up in bed.

"It's just me," Navarro said.

Nina threw a pillow at him. "Have you ever thought about using the front door? Calling first?"

"Can't use the front door," he said, jumping from the sill to the floor. He sat next to her on the bed. "It's Valentine's house until she figures out where she wants to be. Can't phone because it's 2:00 a.m. and I don't want to wake her. Besides, I love coming in the window. It feels very Romeo and Juliet to me, and you know I love the classics."

"What if I don't like you coming in my room?"

"Then you'll say so. But you never do."

"I'd feel kind of strange, since it's your room," Nina said. "But I guess you're not coming to do your laundry at this hour."

"Oh, no. That's not what's on my mind."

She could see him grinning at her in the soft moonlight streaming in the window. "So what *is* on your mind?"

"You. Always you." He sighed. "It's like a disease, only better, because I will never find the cure. And it makes me feel awesome." He touched her hair, stroking it gently.

"Navarro, I have to leave tomorrow."

He sighed. "I know. I won't have this permanently. But it was fun while it lasted."

"Fun?"

He touched her lips with one finger. "We had some laughs, didn't we?"

She wouldn't exactly call it fun. "I guess so."

"Well, then." He patted her rump under the covers and stood. "Is Valentine taking you to the airport?"

How did he seem to know so much about her? "Yes," she said, frowning at him.

"Well, thanks for helping me find my brother. You were right. He did need his family. We'll take good care of Valentine, by the way." He tipped his hat to her and hopped onto the windowsill. "I could use the front door, but this is the last time I'll have a reason to do this, so for the sake of memories, *au revoir.*"

And then he was gone. Nina heard him mount up, then the sound of horse hooves pounding away. She blinked, listening. "Blast him," she said. "Now I'll never get to sleep!"

Because now her mind was going insane. She'd fallen in love with him, but he certainly didn't seem in love with her. Obviously he'd just ridden away without even fighting about taking her to the airport. Without fighting at all.

He hadn't even tried to make love to her. Hadn't even kissed her.

Navarro had always been huge on kissing.

Something was wrong with this picture, but she couldn't figure out what. "Ar-rgh," she said, flipping her pillow over to the cooler side. "No wonder they call this place Malfunction Junction!"

AT THE AIRPORT Nina kept looking, waiting, for a huge, handsome cowboy to come sweep her off her feet.

There was no one but other passengers. Even so, her eyes couldn't seem to stop searching for him.

"Are you all right?" Valentine asked. "You don't seem quite yourself. You have no focus."

"I'm fine," Nina said, wondering why she suddenly wasn't. She and Navarro had said their goodbyes last night. So why did leaving now seem so traumatic?

"Having second thoughts?" Valentine looked at her curiously.

"No. I know it's the right thing to do. I'll feel better when I get back home into my own world, librarian mode. You know," she said, "the strange thing about being here is that the outside world sort of ceases to matter. It would be painful to live at that ranch if one wasn't happy."

"I'm staying. I like it. And I can't wait to start my new job. I'm going to figure out baking. They say that the shop will probably have to change hands in a few years. Maybe if I work real hard…"

Nina smiled, listening to her sister's dreams.

"Everything turned out for the best,"

Nina told her, giving her sister one last hug before she walked through the security check.

"YOU LET HER GO?" Crockett asked. "What are you smoking? You love that gal!"

"Yeah," Navarro said, "but I was just an affair for her. She'll probably go back home and find her an academic sort with glasses and a navy blazer to make her life complete. In that stupid bed, which probably doesn't work worth a flip anyway."

"Not by the time Bloodthirsty got through with it." Crockett shook his head. "Well, if Valentine is in her first trimester, you might see Nina again in, oh, the fall, I suppose."

"Maybe." He didn't care to think about it. Once Nina had told him last night that she was leaving, he'd given up the chase. If she wanted to go that badly, then that's what she needed to do.

He was all for the chase, but it needed to be mutual or then it was just a hunt.

"Hunts are no fun," he told Crockett.

"Depends on what you're bagging."

"Unwilling female."

"Nope," Crockett said. "Unwilling female would not be worth bagging. The very thought gives me shivers."

"Exactly." Navarro turned away and went to ride fence. He wasn't going to think about what could have been, and what turned out to be nothing at all.

Chapter Fifteen

Four months later

"Excuse me, miss," a masculine voice said. "I'd like to check out this book about Curious George."

Nina looked up with a shock of recognition. "Navarro!"

He laughed. "In the flesh."

Nina felt happier and brighter than she had in weeks. "I'm so glad to see you."

"Well, it's a long way to come for a library book, but Curious George is worth it." He handed her the book and his library card.

"Newly issued, I see."

"Absolutely. From the library with the prettiest girls in Delaware."

Nina thought he was flattering her until she saw Colette walk by and give him a wink. Since Colette was a real-life version of Audrey Hepburn, Nina knew Navarro wasn't just trying to butter her up.

With some irritation, she ran his book through the machine and put a card in the pocket. "It's all yours for two weeks."

"Thank you. Want to show me the stacks?"

"All older material is in the basement. Feel free to help yourself."

"I might get lost."

Nina sighed. "If you're here, there are only two reasons that I can think of. Either you want to talk about family stuff or…it's something about us."

"You said there was no us."

Nina blinked. "I guess not."

"So that would be a fool's errand, wouldn't it?" He grinned down at her confidently. Then he tugged her bun gently. "I have it on good authority that men have librarian fantasies."

"I wouldn't know." Nina took the next patron's books and checked them out.

"I'll have to make sure you remember better next time," Navarro said. "Do you want to go out for dinner?"

Of course she did. She'd missed him like crazy. But he'd let her walk out of his life too easily.

Actually, he'd let her do exactly what she'd wanted. Which had taught her a hard lesson about leaving a good man behind and how lonely it could be to be "right." She'd been totally unable to forget him.

He was a true cowboy, and she'd gotten totally caught.

"Let me get this straight. You wanted me to come home and moon over you for four months." Nina tapped her fingernails on the library desk.

"Sounds good so far," Navarro said with a grin.

"Then when I realized just how empty my life was, I'd be so happy you finally showed up that I'd jump into your arms and move to Texas to calcify on your ranch."

"We're far too busy to calcify," Navarro said, "if you hadn't noticed. Of course, librarians may not have the best powers of observation. But," he said, clearly pitying her, "Mimi's baby is growing like a weed, and Last is a new man. I told my brothers to lay off him, and they have, and now we're all looking forward to our bouncing bundle of joy.

"Valentine is dating a guy in town when she can. Mostly she comes home too tired to do anything other than fix some soup and go to bed. We try to get her to eat with us, and sometimes she does, but she likes to unwind in the privacy of what she calls a fabulous house. She loves it. In fact, Valentine and Mimi have struck up a huge friendship. For the first time in a while, there's a woman around our parts for Mimi to pal around with. I have to say the change is incredible. Valentine's pretty feminine, you know, and sometimes I think Mimi's taking lessons."

Nina blinked.

"Mimi pretty much tried to keep up with us while we were growing up. And Lord only knows, she learned an unattractive trait or two. She can outspit Mason with tobacco, for starters."

"Mimi does not dip," Nina said.

"Not with the baby," Navarro said hurriedly. "I meant, in our younger days. Before we all gave up the brown ground leaves of 'baccy."

Nina sighed and checked out another customer. "Thank you, Mrs. Weaver," she said. "See you next time."

"So, you were going to tell me why there's no such thing as a real card catalog system anymore," Navarro said with interest. "And you were going to teach me how the library of the twenty-first century operates. You know, I might volunteer here while I'm in Delaware."

"Oh?" Nina looked at him, wondering where he was going with that. "Planning on staying long?"

"Yep." Navarro grinned. "I know that'll make you happy."

She glanced down at the calendar on the desk. Each day they'd been apart had been marked off with a blue marker. "I didn't miss you much," she said.

"Oh, Nina," an elderly lady said who brought her books to the counter, "is *this* your cowboy?"

"And you tell heap big fib'um," he said, playfully tweaking her nose.

Nina could feel her blush go up her neck. "Mrs. Smith, this is Navarro Jefferson. Navarro, Mrs. Patience Smith."

"Oh, I remember that name," Mrs. Smith said with a big smile for Navarro. "We've heard it so often it's fairly engraved upon our memories." She patted Navarro's arm. "Not that it's a usual name, of course. One pays more attention to unusual names. Particularly as Nina never talked about a man before she met you. Our reading circle has heard all about your wonderful exploits," Mrs. Smith said with a sigh. "We're trying to talk Nina into writing a romance novel about the whole exciting affair."

Navarro smiled at Nina. For the first time ever, Nina wished Mrs. Smith was a tad less friendly. "Isn't she sweet?" she said to Navarro.

"Quite wonderful, and so informative, too. I find the older, more experienced population has a lot of valuable insight and wisdom to impart to us younger folk. Nina, maybe you should consider writing a romance."

"Of course," Mrs. Smith said, her eyes alight with mischief. "Four months is too long to wait before the hero shows up."

"I just think you should know, Mrs. Smith," he said, taking her hand gently in his, "that in Nina's dry-run, first-time-try romance, she had the hero and heroine stay apart for six years. And they were unhappily married to other people."

"Really?" Mrs. Smith looked at Nina. "You always said love at first sight was the best thing that could ever happen to a person. But maybe that doesn't work as well on a blank page," she said philosophically.

"Love at first sight, huh?" Navarro said to Nina.

Nina raised her chin. "Don't get cocky."

"Nina reads to us," Mrs. Smith continued happily. "In our reading circle, a lot of the ladies can no longer see. Some have macular degeneration. So we like to ride the old-lady van and come down here for story time. Nina dresses up like—"

"Mrs. Piggle-Wiggle. I know." Navarro grinned at Nina. "And one day, I want to see that. I have fond memories of Mrs. Piggle-Wiggle myself."

"No," Mrs. Smith said, tapping his arm. "That's how Nina dresses for the children. For us, she dresses as different movie stars of the silver screen, first ladies of eras gone by, and important female personas. We try to guess and then she gives us a history lesson. It's almost like our own college lecture," Mrs. Smith said, beaming. "And then she reads us a classic. Nina's very patient with our love of classic literature."

The smile had left Navarro's face. "I bet she is," he said sincerely. "Nina has a good heart."

Nina checked out another client.

"So, are you taking our girl away from us?" Mrs. Smith whispered when she thought Nina was too busy to hear.

"No," Navarro said. "I'm just here to check out a book."

Nina's heart seemed to break, though after Navarro left, she couldn't say why she hadn't expected it all along.

"Dinner?" Navarro asked as Nina walked outside onto the library steps.

"No librarian worth the fantasy ever turns down dinner with a handsome male," Nina said, keeping her stride even.

Navarro caught up. "It's beautiful here."

"Yes, it is."

"Do I get to see your apartment?"

"Yes," Nina said with a smile. "You

get to see my apartment. And a few other things."

"Oh, goodie," Navarro said. "I love seeing other things."

They boarded a bus, and Nina paid his fare.

"I can do that," he said with surprise.

"You don't know how," she told him. "Shoeshine Johnson's bus never charges the Jefferson boys. Was it you who told me that or Crockett?"

"I don't know." Navarro shrugged and sat down. He stared at the streets as the bus drove on, amazed by the difference in colors, tones and vegetation.

"So why are you here?" Nina asked.

"To get to know the real you," he said sincerely. "I felt like something was missing."

She nodded. "Thank you for only waiting four months. I was afraid of the six-year curse."

"No." Navarro shook his head. "Life's too short."

They got out on the block where Nina's apartment was and walked to it.

"City girl," Navarro said.

Nina laughed. "Not really. Maybe when I move to New York."

"New York?" Navarro sounded shocked.

"Well, it was once a dream of mine." Nina opened the door and two cats rushed out. "I promised to show you some things," she said, "and these are Thing One and Thing Two."

"Oh," Navarro said. "You aren't the things I was hoping to see in Nina's apartment, but hello Thing One and Thing Two." He bent to stroke them as they brushed up against his boots.

"You probably smell very good to them," Nina said. "Where are you taking me to dinner?"

"Someplace quiet." Navarro looked around the apartment. "Lots of greens, very tidy, very homey. I like it, but it's too small."

Nina smiled. "Come see my bedroom."

"Yes, ma'am," Navarro said, following her.

In the center of the bedroom, the charmed heirloom bed was standing beautiful once again. "I love classics," Nina said. "And wonderful old things."

"It looks right in here," Navarro said. "Something was missing about it down in Lonely Hearts Station."

"I shouldn't have let Valentine take it. But she was using it in her apartment next door, and I agreed that she would need a bed in Texas and—you know the story from there." She smiled at Navarro. "Thanks for helping me win it back."

"Maybe I should write a romance novel about that," Navarro said. "I'm going to need a job while I'm here."

"You'll never make it. You'd be as out of place off the ranch as this bed was at Marvella's." She ran a hand lovingly over the wooden headboard. "This bed has had some adventures. If only it could talk."

Navarro sat and the cats jumped into his lap. "I've been thinking about your fear of horses."

Nina walked into the bathroom to change, closing the door. "After Bloodthirsty, I shouldn't be afraid anymore, but the fact is, I'm not cut out for ranch life."

"I reluctantly agree. So I was wondering if you wanted to elope."

Nina opened the bathroom door to stare at him. "Elope?"

"Elope."

"Me and you."

Navarro nodded. "Yes. As in, get married. *That* kind of eloping. By the way, black is my favorite color because of the bra and panties you had on the first time we were together." He looked smug. "You think I'm not a romantic, but the truth is, you're kind of afraid to look below the surface. What are you running from?"

Nina blinked. "Is this a proposal here or a moment of truth?"

"With you, it has to be both. It's best for me to think on dual levels to keep your interest."

"Hence an elopement proposal."

"Well, you seem to like adventure. Something you can write about one day. And I fully expect you to write about everything you learn from me. We're good together. We're a story."

Nina tossed on a robe and came out of the bathroom. "Navarro, where would we live? If we get past the elopement, that is."

He pulled her into his lap, which startled

the cats and made them flee to the windowsill. "I say we drive to Las Vegas, because I've always wanted to see the desert. Then we come back here and find a house in the country. And not just any old house, but one in a rural area with some land. Not too far that you can't drive in to the library to take care of your reading population, because it would be wrong to remove the source of so much pleasure from so many people. But in honor of your fear of horses, I would like to start a horse farm."

Nina blinked. "For me."

"Well, for me. But you made me think of it. I'd like to put together a place where kids can come to ride for lessons and summer camps. I'd like to hire people experienced in hippotherapy for those who need it, like the clinics they have around Dallas. I'd like to do some breeding, try my hand at that." He ran a hand down her robe, admiring the softness and roundness of her body. "Mostly, I need to be with you, and I'm not too proud to say so."

"Why did you let me go if you felt this way?"

Navarro kissed her gently on the lips,

and she kissed him back, experimentally at first, trying to see if the feeling she'd remembered was still there when they touched.

To her delight, Navarro in her arms felt better than ever.

"You needed time to miss me," he said, "and I needed time to face up to the fact that I'd finally fallen in love. I needed to give up my twin and my family for a lusty book lady. Plus, I'm a planning kind of guy. You don't think I thought of this all in one day, do you?"

"Maybe it's too much," Nina said worriedly. "Too much for you to give up."

"It's just enough," Navarro said, "because you made me believe in romantic love. And this bed is going to make sure I get lots of little riders." Winking, he patted the bed and then Nina's fanny. "Do you still believe in love at first sight?"

Nina smiled with joy, opening her arms to him. "More than ever," she said, holding him close, "because I fell in love with you."

Epilogue

When Nina agreed to elope with Navarro, she misunderstood the gravity of the undertaking.

First, he drove the entire trip in her Jeep Cherokee, with new maps he'd downloaded from the computers in the library. This, he said, alleviated the only thing they were ever going to fight about in their marriage, since she knew he was peculiar about maps.

Which meant Nina had to give up something she was peculiar about and that was letting him hold her feet. It was hard to do, but Navarro told her she had feet that fit in the palm of his hand, and, after a while, Nina relaxed and even decided she liked it. Even more, she liked cooking worldwide cuisine in the old barn they'd converted into a wonderful home. Nina cooked wearing Chinese sandals, an apron that said Feed Your Mind A Book, and not much else, an occurrence that assured her of Navarro's rapt attention.

They discovered they had many things in common.

Thing One and Thing Two were impressed with the barn in the Delaware countryside. There were plenty of little field mice to chase, and the cats loved making beds in the hay, so they were very content.

Navarro arranged for the "old people" van to bring Nina's reading circle to the ranch twice a month, so they could enjoy the nice air in the countryside and have Nina read to them in the massive library he put in on the ground floor so they wouldn't have to climb stairs. She could also do more elaborate costume recitals for them in the gazebo he built out in the yard, and these recitals were so much enjoyed by everyone—including Mrs. Patience Smith—that Nina's performances were soon requested by the general public.

Navarro renamed the van the Curious

George Mobile, because he said no one was ever too old to enjoy a good book. When he drove the van, he wore a big yellow hat Nina said only he could wear so well.

The children also got to visit twice a month in the Curious George Mobile, but they were more interested in the ponies and horses Navarro had purchased than the books, so Nina had to be more creative with her efforts. Her husband, she learned, was an intellectual force in his own right. He bought a wagon and taught the children Latin as he rode them around the pasture. The children were so fascinated by the size of the Suffolk Punch pulling the wagon that they happily learned Latin to earn their rides.

Navarro so loved it when Nina dressed up like Mrs. Piggle-Wiggle that he made his own pirate costume, reminiscent of Mrs. Piggle-Wiggle's husband who had many chests of gold hidden in his home. Nina loved her sexy Navarro in pirate gear and never made him walk the plank.

As for the charmed bed, it resided on the third floor where the nursery would one day be. The bed had yet live up to its legend—but Nina and Navarro made lots of opportunities for the family fairy tale to come true.

* * * * *

YES! Please send me the *Cowboy at Heart* collection in Larger Print. This collection begins with 3 FREE books and 2 FREE gifts in the first shipment, and more free gifts will follow! My books will arrive in 8 monthly shipments until I have the entire 51-book *Cowboy at Heart* collection. I will receive 2 or 3 FREE books in each shipment and I will pay just $4.99 U.S./ $5.89 CDN. for each of the other four books in each shipment, plus $2.99 for shipping and handling.* If I decide to keep the entire collection, I'll have paid for only 32 books because 19 books are FREE! I understand that by accepting the 3 free books and gifts places me under no obligation to buy anything. I can always return a shipment and cancel at any time. My free books and gifts are mine to keep no matter what I decide.

256 HCN 0779   456 HCN 0779

Name	(PLEASE PRINT)	
Address		Apt. #
City	State/Prov.	Zip/Postal Code

Signature (if under 18, a parent or guardian must sign)

Mail to the Harlequin® Reader Service:

IN U.S.A.: P.O. Box 1867, Buffalo, NY 14240-1867
IN CANADA: P.O. Box 609, Fort Erie, Ontario L2A 5X3

* Terms and prices subject to change without notice. Prices do not include applicable taxes. Sales tax applicable in N.Y. Canadian residents will be charged applicable taxes. This offer is limited to one order per household. All orders subject to approval. Credit or debit balances in a customer's account(s) may be offset by any other outstanding balance owed by or to the customer. Please allow 4 to 6 weeks for delivery. Offer available while quantities last. Offer not available to Quebec residents.

CAHBPA13

REQUEST YOUR FREE BOOKS!
2 FREE NOVELS PLUS 2 FREE GIFTS!

HARLEQUIN®

American ★ Romance®

LOVE, HOME & HAPPINESS

YES! Please send me 2 FREE Harlequin® American Romance® novels and my 2 FREE gifts (gifts are worth about $10). After receiving them, if I don't wish to receive any more books, I can return the shipping statement marked "cancel." If I don't cancel, I will receive 4 brand-new novels every month and be billed just $4.49 per book in the U.S. or $5.24 per book in Canada. That's a savings of at least 14% off the cover price! It's quite a bargain! Shipping and handling is just 50¢ per book in the U.S. and 75¢ per book in Canada.* I understand that accepting the 2 free books and gifts places me under no obligation to buy anything. I can always return a shipment and cancel at any time. Even if I never buy another book, the two free books and gifts are mine to keep forever.

154/354 HDN FV47

Name	(PLEASE PRINT)	

Address		Apt. #

City	State/Prov.	Zip/Postal Code

Signature (if under 18, a parent or guardian must sign)

Mail to the Harlequin® Reader Service:
IN U.S.A.: P.O. Box 1867, Buffalo, NY 14240-1867
IN CANADA: P.O. Box 609, Fort Erie, Ontario L2A 5X3

Want to try two free books from another line?
Call 1-800-873-8635 or visit www.ReaderService.com.

* Terms and prices subject to change without notice. Prices do not include applicable taxes. Sales tax applicable in N.Y. Canadian residents will be charged applicable taxes. Offer not valid in Quebec. This offer is limited to one order per household. Not valid for current subscribers to Harlequin American Romance books. All orders subject to credit approval. Credit or debit balances in a customer's account(s) may be offset by any other outstanding balance owed by or to the customer. Please allow 4 to 6 weeks for delivery. Offer available while quantities last.

Your Privacy—The Harlequin® Reader Service is committed to protecting your privacy. Our Privacy Policy is available online at www.ReaderService.com or upon request from the Harlequin Reader Service.

We make a portion of our mailing list available to reputable third parties that offer products we believe may interest you. If you prefer that we not exchange your name with third parties, or if you wish to clarify or modify your communication preferences, please visit us at www.ReaderService.com/consumerschoice or write to us at Harlequin Reader Service Preference Service, P.O. Box 9062, Buffalo, NY 14269. Include your complete name and address.

HARDIR13

REQUEST YOUR FREE BOOKS!
2 FREE NOVELS PLUS 2 FREE GIFTS!

✦ HARLEQUIN®

SPECIAL EDITION

Life, Love & Family

YES! Please send me 2 FREE Harlequin® Special Edition novels and my 2 FREE gifts (gifts are worth about $10). After receiving them, if I don't wish to receive any more books, I can return the shipping statement marked "cancel." If I don't cancel, I will receive 6 brand-new novels every month and be billed just $4.49 per book in the U.S. or $5.24 per book in Canada. That's a savings of at least 14% off the cover price! It's quite a bargain! Shipping and handling is just 50¢ per book in the U.S. and 75¢ per book in Canada.* I understand that accepting the 2 free books and gifts places me under no obligation to buy anything. I can always return a shipment and cancel at any time. Even if I never buy another book, the two free books and gifts are mine to keep forever.

235/335 HDN FV4K

Name	(PLEASE PRINT)

Address	Apt. #

City	State/Prov.	Zip/Postal Code

Signature (if under 18, a parent or guardian must sign)

Mail to the Harlequin® Reader Service:
IN U.S.A.: P.O. Box 1867, Buffalo, NY 14240-1867
IN CANADA: P.O. Box 609, Fort Erie, Ontario L2A 5X3

Want to try two free books from another line?
Call 1-800-873-8635 or visit www.ReaderService.com.

* Terms and prices subject to change without notice. Prices do not include applicable taxes. Sales tax applicable in N.Y. Canadian residents will be charged applicable taxes. Offer not valid in Quebec. This offer is limited to one order per household. Not valid for current subscribers to Harlequin Special Edition books. All orders subject to credit approval. Credit or debit balances in a customer's account(s) may be offset by any other outstanding balance owed by or to the customer. Please allow 4 to 6 weeks for delivery. Offer available while quantities last.

Your Privacy—The Harlequin® Reader Service is committed to protecting your privacy. Our Privacy Policy is available online at www.ReaderService.com or upon request from the Harlequin Reader Service.

We make a portion of our mailing list available to reputable third parties that offer products we believe may interest you. If you prefer that we not exchange your name with third parties, or if you wish to clarify or modify your communication preferences, please visit us at www.ReaderService.com/consumerschoice or write to us at Harlequin Reader Service Preference Service, P.O. Box 9062, Buffalo, NY 14269. Include your complete name and address.

HSEDIR13

REQUEST YOUR FREE BOOKS!
2 FREE NOVELS PLUS 2 FREE GIFTS!

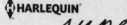

HARLEQUIN® *super romance*®

Exciting, emotional, unexpected!

YES! Please send me 2 FREE Harlequin® Superromance® novels and my 2 FREE gifts (gifts are worth about $10). After receiving them, if I don't wish to receive any more books, I can return the shipping statement marked "cancel." If I don't cancel, I will receive 6 brand-new novels every month and be billed just $4.69 per book in the U.S. or $5.24 per book in Canada. That's a savings of at least 15% off the cover price! It's quite a bargain! Shipping and handling is just 50¢ per book in the U.S. and 75¢ per book in Canada.* I understand that accepting the 2 free books and gifts places me under no obligation to buy anything. I can always return a shipment and cancel at any time. Even if I never buy another book, the two free books and gifts are mine to keep forever.

135/336 HDN FV5K

Name _____ (PLEASE PRINT)

Address _____ Apt. #

City _____ State/Prov. _____ Zip/Postal Code

Signature (if under 18, a parent or guardian must sign)

Mail to the **Harlequin®** Reader Service:
IN U.S.A.: P.O. Box 1867, Buffalo, NY 14240-1867
IN CANADA: P.O. Box 609, Fort Erie, Ontario L2A 5X3

**Are you a current subscriber to Harlequin Superromance books and want to receive the larger-print edition?
Call 1-800-873-8635 or visit www.ReaderService.com.**

* Terms and prices subject to change without notice. Prices do not include applicable taxes. Sales tax applicable in N.Y. Canadian residents will be charged applicable taxes. Offer not valid in Quebec. This offer is limited to one order per household. Not valid for current subscribers to Harlequin Superromance books. All orders subject to credit approval. Credit or debit balances in a customer's account(s) may be offset by any other outstanding balance owed by or to the customer. Please allow 4 to 6 weeks for delivery. Offer available while quantities last.

Your Privacy—The Harlequin® Reader Service is committed to protecting your privacy. Our Privacy Policy is available online at www.ReaderService.com or upon request from the Harlequin Reader Service.

We make a portion of our mailing list available to reputable third parties that offer products we believe may interest you. If you prefer that we not exchange your name with third parties, or if you wish to clarify or modify your communication preferences, please visit us at www.ReaderService.com/consumerschoice or write to us at Harlequin Reader Service Preference Service, P.O. Box 9062, Buffalo, NY 14269. Include your complete name and address.

REQUEST YOUR FREE BOOKS!

 HARLEQUIN® HISTORICAL:
Where love is timeless

2 FREE NOVELS PLUS 2 **FREE GIFTS!**

YES! Please send me 2 FREE Harlequin® Historical novels and my 2 FREE gifts (gifts are worth about $10). After receiving them, if I don't wish to receive any more books, I can return the shipping statement marked "cancel." If I don't cancel, I will receive 6 brand-new novels every month and be billed just $5.19 per book in the U.S. or $5.74 per book in Canada. That's a savings of at least 17% off the cover price! It's quite a bargain! Shipping and handling is just 50¢ per book in the U.S. and 75¢ per book in Canada.* I understand that accepting the 2 free books and gifts places me under no obligation to buy anything. I can always return a shipment and cancel at any time. Even if I never buy another book, the two free books and gifts are mine to keep forever.

246/349 HDN FV3V

Name	(PLEASE PRINT)

Address	Apt. #

City	State/Prov.	Zip/Postal Code

Signature (if under 18, a parent or guardian must sign)

Mail to the **Harlequin®** Reader Service:
IN U.S.A.: P.O. Box 1867, Buffalo, NY 14240-1867
IN CANADA: P.O. Box 609, Fort Erie, Ontario L2A 5X3

Want to try two free books from another line?
Call 1-800-873-8635 or visit www.ReaderService.com.

* Terms and prices subject to change without notice. Prices do not include applicable taxes. Sales tax applicable in N.Y. Canadian residents will be charged applicable taxes. Offer not valid in Quebec. This offer is limited to one order per household. Not valid for current subscribers to Harlequin Historical books. All orders subject to credit approval. Credit or debit balances in a customer's account(s) may be offset by any other outstanding balance owed by or to the customer. Please allow 4 to 6 weeks for delivery. Offer available while quantities last.

Your Privacy—The Harlequin® Reader Service is committed to protecting your privacy. Our Privacy Policy is available online at www.ReaderService.com or upon request from the Harlequin Reader Service.

We make a portion of our mailing list available to reputable third parties that offer products we believe may interest you. If you prefer that we not exchange your name with third parties, or if you wish to clarify or modify your communication preferences, please visit us at www.ReaderService.com/consumerschoice or write to us at Harlequin Reader Service Preference Service, P.O. Box 9062, Buffalo, NY 14269. Include your complete name and address.

HHDIR13